MW01251104

don't call me daughter

The Bassett Hound Chronicles
Book One

Patricia J Childers

Copyright © 2022 by Patricia Jean Childers

Interior design by P J Childers
Book Cover by P J Childers
Mistakes by P J Childers

ISBN 979-8-9869435-1-0 Hardcover
ISBN 979-8-9869435-0-3 Softcover
ISBN 979-8-9869435-2-7 ebook

foggy bottom B books

DEDICATIONS

It takes a village to raise a child. And it takes a village, a husband, two children, a few solid friends, a Bassett hound, and two years to write a book. I thought it would be a whole lot easier. The author is incredibly grateful for the support of the following people (alphabetically):

Chris Childers

Cory Cosman

Petra Craddock

Kipp Euler

Christi Gibson

Brooke Jones

Hunter, the Bassett Hound, Muse

Perry Mason, Story Consultant

don't call me daughter

Chapter 1
Ray Flynn and what he saw
Sunday/Monday Morning

The first shot of whiskey was harsh. The second was smoother. The third brought the calmness Ray Flynn so desperately needed. He sat on a tall stool at Jake's, hunched over the wooden bar, hands trembling, heart beating like a trip hammer. Overwhelmed.

Earlier that afternoon, he had been fishing along the shore of the Altamaha River. The fish were not biting and the hot, afternoon sun made him drowsy. He could barely keep his eyes open. He decided to leave his line in the water while he nodded off. With a long, sure cast, he landed the bait in the middle of the river where the current ran the fastest. He waited for the line to tighten, and anchored the rod between two large rocks. He leaned against a tree and slid the bill of his cap down until it touched his nose, then fell asleep.

A loud splash woke him. He was not alone. He carefully moved the bill of his cap above his eyes so he could see what was happening. He saw two men struggling with a large, heavy object on the shoreline a short distance away. They dragged it, arranged it, and seemed intent on dumping it into the river. He was pretty sure the object was a body, and from the pink fabric that trailed behind it, maybe female.

He sat as still as possible, wishing he was invisible. The two men were easier to see now. They stood up on the shore and watched the last evidence of the body submerge into the dark water. Circles on the water's surface above it widened until they disappeared entirely. It was as if it never happened.

Curiosity quickly turned to fear when he realized he had just watched two men dispose of a body in the river. If they had any idea he was there, he would be next. Plan A was to wait them out and leave after they were gone. There was no Plan B.

Suddenly his rod jumped clear off the rocks, clacking loudly as it hurtled toward the water, chasing the fish at the other end of the line. The men immediately turned toward the sound, and ran in his direction. Terrified, he stood up in one move and pulled his hat down over his face. With several long strides he was beyond the trees and across the road. He didn't stop walking until he reached Jake's.

Jake's Bar felt like a safe haven to Ray. Everything was familiar, everyone was familiar. After gulping the shots down, he switched to Jack Daniels and coke. It warmed his insides and numbed his brain. He drank slowly until he started to breathe normally. The liquor didn't solve his problems, but it did help cushion them.

Around supper time, Larry came in and sat next to him. He trusted Larry, and he told him everything. His friend listened silently. It was apparent Ray's life was in danger, which meant anyone he talked to was in danger, too. Larry wiped his mouth on the bottom of his shirt, slid off the stool, and limped out of the bar. Self-preservation.

By ten o'clock, the whiskey had affected Ray's balance. He was banking off the walls to the bathroom like a billiard ball in a game of pool. He stopped drinking but the damage was done. When his head grew too heavy to hold up, it landed face-first on the bar where he fell into a dreamless sleep.

Jake shook him awake at closing time. He had finished the

evening chores. The chairs were turned over on the tables, glasses washed, and floor swept. "Time to go home," he told him.

Ray opened his eyes, then raised his head off the bar. His head was throbbing and he could hear his heartbeat in his ears. He wiped the drool from his mouth with the back of his hand, and rubbed it on his pants. When he remembered the men and the body, his heart felt like it flipped over and his hands started shaking. He didn't think the men had a good look at him, but he would have to be very careful. Stay under the radar. Right now, he just wanted to go home and sleep in his bed.

"I'm awake," he said, sitting up. He tried to stand when he got off the bar stool, but his legs felt boneless, sending him sprawling onto the floor. Jake helped him up.

"This isn't like you, Ray. What's up?"

He thought about telling Jake. "You wouldn't believe what I saw," he said, instead.

"What'd you see?"

He didn't know who to trust. "You wouldn't believe it."

Jake laughed. "You're right. I probably wouldn't."

Ray was up and moving toward the door. Home was a short walk away. He stumbled into the dark night, sidewalks framed with gaslights to light the way. When he reached his house, he could hear Walter howling for him. He smiled, and turned the key in the doorknob until the door opened. The Bassett Hound bellowed louder. He squatted down to rub the dog's ears. "It's okay, Walter. I'm home."

But the dog wasn't looking at him anymore. Walter was focused on something behind him. Aware that he hadn't heard the door close behind him, Ray stood up slowly. Before he could turn and look, a hand covered his mouth and jerked his head back. In the final seconds of his life, Ray remembered he left his tackle box with his fishing license behind the tree.

Walter threw his head back and howled

Chapter 2
The Armstrong Funeral Home
Tuesday

Ella Flynn's father was dead. The Coroner for Wayne County called her with the news. Early that morning, Ray Flynn had been found deceased on the sofa in his residence in Prosper, Georgia. The initial cause of death was ruled natural causes, the Coroner told her, and his body had been taken to Savannah for an autopsy. After that surprising phone call, the funeral director of the Armstrong Funeral Home called. He asked Ella to come to Prosper, if she could, to finalize funeral arrangements.

Although it wasn't something she wanted to do, it was definitely something she thought she should do. Ella was a Chicago Police Department detective, assigned to the Violent Crimes Unit, in the middle of an investigation into the death of an Alderman's son. Most leaves had been cancelled because of their heavy workload, but Chief Warner gave her a "generous" two-day bereavement leave. She hoped she'd only need one day. Arrive on Tuesday, fly back to Chicago on Wednesday.

Tuesday morning, Ella caught an early bird flight to Atlanta out of Chicago's O'Hare Airport, rented a car, and drove to her father's hometown in Southeastern Georgia. It was a long drive, the land was flat, the sun was hot. She was bored.

Everything about the little town of Prosper was mediocre. The houses were no larger than they needed to be and squatted on small lots. Gardens held a few flowers, but no more than absolutely necessary. The roads were pitted and rough, and the retail shops hovered together in a frantic mosaic of differing styles. Bars and liquor stores were abundant, though, and well-advertised.

The dirt was red. For someone from the Midwest, this was the absolute wrong color. Dirt is brown, unless it's covered by snow, then it's gray. Ella was suspicious of red clay.

Her GPS told her to turn right at the next road, Second Street, and there it was, the most unlikely house in town. It was a stunning Queen Anne Victorian-style house that had somehow morphed into the Armstrong Funeral Home. Decorated with at least five colors, it featured a turret, and a white wraparound verandah showcasing pots of colorful flowers dripping from the roof. In the shade, by the front window, an inviting cushioned swing resided, rocking with the breeze. It reminded her of simpler times.

Ella parked and flipped the mirror down in the car to check her face. There was no spinach in her teeth and her nose looked clean. Along with her white Chicago Cubs baseball hat, with her dark hair trailing out of the hole in the back, there were big sunglasses. No one would be overwhelmed by her appearance, but nobody would scream in horror, either. She hoped.

A brass knocker on the heavy wooden doors beckoned, and she used it liberally to announce her arrival. The sound echoed loudly, so she did it twice. The second time because she was hot. When the big double-doors opened, Ella was hit by the fragrance of potpourri and incense. She liked the smell, even though she knew the scents were used to mask the odor of embalming fluid.

The greeter's name was Martha and she was vintage to match the house. She had light gray hair with a blue shine like car wax, and her eyebrows were drawn on in arcs that made her seem surprised to see you. Her smile was genuine. The décor inside the large funeral home was understated, refined, but still lush. Ella approved. Period antique furniture filled the foyer and displayed discreet boxes of tissues, conveniently placed for mourners.

In hushed tones, Ella explained the reason for her visit to Martha, who nodded and ushered her down a long, narrow entry hall with four sets of pocket doors on either side. They led into a pair of double parlors, closed today.

Their destination was the library, which included a very long antique wooden table, hundreds of books in floor-to-ceiling bookcases, and flowery wallpaper. Three very large paintings of sour-looking old men glared down on the room from above the wainscoting. The effect was both frightening and funny, and Ella wasn't sure why. The breeze from the ceiling paddle fan flirted with wisps of her hair, and tickled her nose. She sneezed.

Martha pointed out a wooden chair at the head of the table, and Ella sat down. Then, promising sweet tea on her return, she left through a door that seemed to lead to the kitchen at the back of the home.

Ella made herself comfortable, taking off her Chicago Cubs hat and sunglasses and laying them on the table. She glanced sideways at the hat, and picked it back up. It was an old friend, given to her years ago. It was white with a large blue C on the front. She rubbed a little dirt off the crown. The bill was dark red, shiny from use, edges soft and frayed, properly curved like a duck's bill. She laid it back down reverently. It wasn't just a hat; her mother gave it to her and that made it irreplaceable. The room was quiet. She rested her back against the cushioned chair and closed her eyes.

When her mother died last year, she had to meet with the funeral director in Berwyn to make the arrangements. It was horribly sad, and to this day, she cried when she thought about it. Ella tried to feel something like sorrow or regret about her father's death. There was nothing there. He left them more than twenty years ago. Was he tall or short? To a little girl, everyone was tall. Her mother's eyes had been hazel, but Ella's eyes were light brown. Did he have brown eyes, too? She couldn't remember.

A door at the back of the room opened and Martha returned with a pitcher of tea. She was followed by a tall man about Ella's age, dressed casually in a white shirt with sleeves rolled above his elbows and a tie loosely worn below his collar. Hands in his pockets. Black slacks. Scuffed loafers, no socks. He wore glasses with black frames. Ella didn't wear glasses, but she thought it was just a matter of time. It had become harder to read.

"Here you are," Martha said. She carefully set the pitcher down onto a silver platter. The sweet tea was filled with slices of lemon making Ella's mouth water. She eagerly watched Martha pour two tall glasses full.

"Jackson Lee Armstrong," the man behind Martha said, confidently. "I'm the funeral director of the Armstrong Funeral Home here. Thanks so much for coming."

She stood up to shake his hand. "Nice to meet you, Jackson," she said. "My name is Ella Flynn, from Chicago, but you know that." She felt under-dressed in her tan khaki pants and hi-top sneakers. He had kept her hand, which she reluctantly took back. She noticed he had just enough sexy chin stubble to avoid appearing homeless.

"The name is Jackson Lee, ma'am," he said with a smile. This is the South after all. Everybody has two first names." He winked at her.

"Mine is Ella," she smiled, and winked back.

He laughed. "Lovely name, Ella. Please sit down and make yourself comfortable." She quickly complied, and he handed a glass of sweet tea to her.

He absently ran his fingers through his hair as he sat down beside her. "Thank you so much for coming on such short notice." He glanced over at her Chicago Cubs hat on the table. "Baseball fan?"

She nodded her head and smiled. "Big baseball fan. Mostly a Chicago Cubs fan. What about you? Do you follow the Atlanta Braves?"

"Yes, I do," he said firmly, with a big smile. "I make sure to get to a game every time I'm in Atlanta and they're at home. I'd love to go to Wrigley Field someday." He pursed his lips in thought. "What's the best baseball movie?" he asked her.

She didn't even have to think about it. "'Major League' for comedy. But I loved 'Bull Durham' for real baseball talk. What about you?"

He raised an eyebrow and pondered the question. "Those are great, but I'm going to have to go with 'The Natural' with Robert Redford." He seemed quite pleased with himself.

Ella laughed. "I'm not sure I can agree with you, Buddy. But I respect your right to be wrong." He laughed, too.

She took a long drink of the cold tea and glanced at Jackson Lee while he was sorting the papers he brought to the table. He had an engaging way of talking that enchanted Ella, with his deep voice and the slow, lazy rhythm of his words. He had a captivating Southern drawl that made her want to hear more.

"I must admit," she said, "this is a beautiful house. It looks like it was imported from Savannah."

He glanced up and smiled, eager to talk about it. "It is spectacular, isn't it? It was built in 1895 for a lumber baron. He was enamored with Savannah houses, so he built this Queen Anne-style house with all the gingerbread it could handle, and a four-sided white wooden porch." He sounded proud. "My grandfather bought it and turned it into the Armstrong Funeral Home. We've lived here for three generations, so far."

She glanced up at the tin ceiling. "It looks just like it must have more than one-hundred years ago. Amazing. And the paintings on the wall? Relatives of yours?"

He turned his attention to the paintings behind him. "Great-grandfather, grandfather, father. They're keeping an eye on me."

"They don't seem happy." They looked uncomfortable.

"I never met my great-grandfather or grandfather. They died when my father was young." He tapped his fingers on the table. "My father took over the family business, and it came to me when he died." He turned back to his paperwork, dismissing the subject.

She was sorry she brought it up, and took another long sip of the tea.

He glanced up again, and this time he studied her. "How was your flight from Chicago? Did you drive from Atlanta, then?"

She thought about the morning drive, considered telling him about how boring it was, then decided to gloss over it. "Why, it was just fine," was what she came up with.

"Glad to hear it. Prosper is easy to find. Just don't go too far or you'll end up in the Altamaha River." She smiled at him and he smiled back, with his perfect, white teeth.

"No trouble at all." She sipped politely from her glass. He wasn't at all like Ella had imagined a funeral director would look like. Much younger. Dark, wavy hair, a little on the long side. With a truly righteous nose. Not so big that it entered the room before he did, and certainly not bulbous in any way. It fit in nicely above his lips, which she liked, too. He was a handsome man.

He laid a few papers on the table. "There are a few things for you to sign since you seem to be Ray Flynn's only heir."

She drank the rest of her iced tea, then watched Jackson Lee fill her glass again. "I guess I am. I don't know what my father has been up to for the past twenty-some years." He could have ten children as far as she knew, but apparently Ella had been the only one they could find. "He left my mother and me when I was seven."

He seemed surprised. "You haven't seen or talked with your father since then?"

"No, I haven't," she admitted. "I knew he went back to his hometown. My mother told me that. But that's about it."

He didn't say anything for a few seconds, just concentrated on shuffling the papers on the table, then turned and looked directly at her. "Sorry. That sucks."

She nodded in agreement.

"I have his wallet to pass on to you," he said, handing her a black wallet.

She took the leather wallet and held it in her hand. When she opened it up, she found a credit card, gas card, and a couple of woodworking business cards with his name and phone number on them. She examined all the hiding spots, but didn't turn anything up. In the section that held currency, there was thirty-six dollars, along with a newspaper clipping. It was about her.

She glanced at Jackson Lee reading through his paperwork. "This is about me," she told him.

"I know," he said, and smiled. "It's how the Coroner found you."

She laid the folded paper on the table and straightened it. The 2014 announcement featured new members of the Chicago Police Department, and a list of their names. She stood in uniform, in the second row. Ella Flynn. Her father had this in his wallet. *He kept it. It was important to him*, she thought. *He didn't forget me.* She put the newspaper clipping back in the wallet just as it had been, and set the wallet gently on the table. It changed the way she felt about him.

"Your father left you a couple of things," Jackson Lee said, sipping his iced tea, putting it back on the puddle it had created on the tray. He rubbed his chin in thought.

"I hope it's a lot of money," she said, facetiously.

"Not much money, and it'll be tied up in the Georgia courts for a while.

"Stamp collection?"

He looked amused. "No. He left you his house. It's paid for."

She was surprised. "I don't want his house," she said, flatly. "I don't mean to be rude, but I have my mother's house in Chicago, and I don't even want that." More stuff.

Jackson Lee shrugged. "It doesn't matter. It's your house now."

She brushed an errant strand of hair back behind her ear. "I suppose I can sell it. I'll see what I can pack up to clean it out." *I should be grateful for having two houses, instead of complaining about it.* "It's good that he left it to me," she said, and smiled. *Grateful is a much better response*, she thought.

"At least it can be a place for you to stay tonight," he suggested. "Are you leaving tomorrow?"

"Yes," she said decisively. "The coroner told me they sent the body to the Georgia Bureau of Investigation in Savannah for an autopsy, which sounds a little much for natural causes. Anyway, the results should be back by tomorrow morning, so I'll wait." She didn't like to do things halfway. She had to know the results before she left.

He sat back in his chair and crossed his leg over his knee, revealing a bare ankle. "It's up to the coroner, but Georgia law says unexplained deaths, with no obvious medical cause, are autopsied, and your father was only fifty-five. They couldn't find any medical history on him at all. Some coroners let it go. This one was just elected so he's sticking by the rules."

Ella understood, as a funeral director, he needed to stay apprised of Georgia county law. Especially since it affected his business. She sat back in her chair, too. "Good to know. In Chicago, we'd let it go."

"That's right," he said. "You work for the Chicago Police Department. You're a detective?" He sat straight, interested. He adjusted his glasses.

"Yes, I'm a detective, assigned to the Violent Crimes Unit." Although she said it in a matter-of-fact tone, it was easy to tell she was proud of her job. "I generally work on new or old homicide cases, robberies, fugitive offenders, gathering evidence or reviewing evidence, working toward a conviction. I've been doing this for about two years now." She sat up a little straighter. "I've been a Chicago cop for eight years."

He was definitely impressed. "You have kind of no-nonsense demeanor that would go with that job." He sat back in his chair with an amused smile.

She liked his insight on her personality. "I take that as a compliment. I guess police officers are a certain type that's universal."

"You don't have the usual police mustache, so that's refreshing." That made her laugh. She enjoyed his subtle humor. "And you're direct. I like that."

She was sure he was flirting with her. "Thanks. Not everybody agrees with you."

"I don't care." He tapped his pen on the table, and smiled at her.

She was pleased. "I will never fit in," she said, proudly. "That's one of my best qualities." She carefully signed each piece of paper, and returned them to him. "You're the nicest funeral director I've ever met." *And the most charming*, she thought.

"How many funeral directors have you met?"

"Including you?" She pursed her lips and thought about it. "Two."

He laughed out loud. "And I'm at the top! High praise. Thank you, ma'am."

The afternoon was lazy and Ella didn't want to leave yet. She was comfortable in her chair. "Being here in his hometown makes my father seem very real to me. I've thought of him as the invisible man for years, as though he didn't exist. Do you know what I mean?" She watched him for a response.

He nodded. "Yes, I do. It's easier to dismiss him when you're hundreds of miles away. Harder to do this when you can see where he lived."

"Exactly. He lived here. You knew him, right?"

"I did."

"Tell me what he looked like." She was anxious to know.

"Good question." He stroked the soft hair on his chin. "He was a little shorter than me, and I'm about six feet tall. So maybe five-foot-ten. Slender. His hair was salt and pepper, close-cut, and he had a full beard. It was a mostly white beard and mustache." He looked at her for approval.

She smiled. "Good enough. Do you think I look like him?"

He gave it some thought, sitting back in his chair and crossing his legs. "There is a definite resemblance, something about your eyes and your smile."

Ella smiled. "He was young when he left us. He had dark hair and a mustache, and he was on the thin side. I wondered what he would look like when he got older."

"He was very friendly," he continued. "Now that it's too late, I would have liked to have gone fishing with him. But I missed my chance." He stared out the window into the garden and thoughtfully rubbed his forehead. "Ray was a woodworker, you know. Cabinet maker and really skilled. But when he was younger, he was the assistant football coach at the high school."

"I like that," she said.

"In fact, he was my high school football coach."

"Really? Was he a good coach?"

"He was a great coach," he said. "My father didn't want me to play football. He was all about studying to get in the best schools and he thought football was a waste of time."

"Isn't that considered a crime in Georgia?" she asked, with a laugh.

He laughed, too. "I hope our secret never gets out. For a tall, skinny guy without much experience or talent, your father was a godsend. Your father knew everything about football. But it was more than the rules and plays. He knew how to get the best from each member of the team. Can I tell you a story?"

"Please do," she said, leaning in.

"It was the next-to-last game of the year, a home game, and we were playing the best team that year, Boone County, on a cold Tuesday night. I wasn't first string. I occupied a warm spot on the bench and hoped I would only have to offer encouragement, and not actual physical participation."

She couldn't help but laugh at his self-deprecating humor. "I'm sure you were better than you remember."

He smiled. "I'd like you to think that I was better than that. But I didn't have a lot of confidence. Or experience."

"I shivered on the bench for three quarters. In the fourth quarter, the score was tied at fourteen with two minutes to go. Boone County had the ball on our thirty-yard line. It was first down. The coach called a timeout. Ray told me I was in the game.

We had to hold Boone County, so I was going in as a linebacker. He put his hands on my shoulders and told me this was the moment we had been training for. It wasn't just up to me. It was up to the team, but I was the most important part of the team because Boone County hadn't seen me play yet. I needed to show them I was to be respected and feared. Because he respected my ability and courage."

"And he made you believe that?" She liked Ray, the coach.

"I knew I could do it. Coach thought I could it. Why else would he put me in?"

She was hooked "And then what happened? Please don't stop."

"We held them at the line of scrimmage. The second down, they gained three yards. The third down, with seven yards to go, their quarterback threw a pass and I intercepted it. It was magical. I tucked it in like it was sewn to my jersey and ran like hell the other way. Somewhere around our forty-yard line, I was knocked off balance and went down like I was shot."

She laughed with him. "That is so awesome!" she exclaimed. "Did you win?"

He smiled. "We did. We won that game. And your father gave me the game ball."

She loved it. "Do you think you could have done it without him?"

He thought it over. "No. He told me what I needed to hear."

She was happy for him. "I really like your story. "I wish I knew my father the way you did. I've been mad at him for a long time." *I'm tired of being mad at him*, she thought. *This would be a good time to stop, now that he's gone.*

She sat back in her chair. The afternoon was delicious. "Did you always want to be a funeral director?"

"No, I never wanted to be a funeral director," he said firmly, looking directly at her. "I went to the University of Georgia and studied Biology. I considered going to Grad school, but decided against it because

I wanted to do something completely different. I joined the Air Force."
He smiled.

"That is so cool," she said, smiling. "I am impressed." Ella knew many veterans. They were attracted to the police force because of what they learned in the military. "What was your specialty?"

"I was a Medical Technician at Khandahar Airfield in Afghanistan."

She nodded. "Wow. How close were you to the front lines?" She would have liked to have joined the Air Force. It fit her like a glove.

"Close enough to get hit by shrapnel." He rolled his eyes behind his glasses. "Too close, I guess."

"Tell me about it. I mean, if you don't mind talking about it." She wanted to know more.

He fidgeted in his chair until he was comfortable, and crossed his legs. "I don't mind talking about it. My job was to provide medical care to all deployed airmen who came through Khandahar. Occasionally, we had to provide medical care in the heat of battle. A homemade bomb in the roadway exploded, and shrapnel hit my thigh, rearranging muscle tissue and bones."

"That sounds pretty awful. How long were you in the hospital?" It sounded like a serious injury.

"A month or two, in Germany. Then I was sent home for rehabilitation. It took a while to get the strength back in my leg." He pointed to the thigh of his left leg.

"I'm sorry that happened to you," she said, sympathetically. "You came back to the funeral home?"

He paused. "My rehab was at Robins Air Force Base, but when my father was sick, I came back here. He died a short time later." He seemed sad, and glanced away from her. He took his glasses off and lay them on the table, then he rubbed his eyes, and put them back on. "He was only fifty-five years old, and I was twenty-eight." He turned back to her. "He made me promise to take over the funeral home and keep it in the family."

She nodded her head. "That's what you did, obviously."

He smiled. "Of course. I went back to school for my degree in Mortuary Science and settled in as the third funeral director in my family. My interests in biology and medical science coincide nicely with mortician duties."

"It's good that you like working with dead bodies. I do, too." They laughed together. "Something in common." Ella was enjoying herself, and Jackson Lee seemed very relaxed.

He smiled again. "It's not a bad life, you know. I'm not unhappy with the way things worked out." He straightened up in his chair and put his hands on his knees. "I'm fine, really. What about you? Did you always want to be a police officer?"

"Bet your ass," she said. "Even when I was little, I was the neighborhood vigilante. When I was eight, I kicked a bully in the nuts." She didn't ask for trouble, but she didn't walk away from it, either.

He laughed so hard, he coughed and had to catch his breath.

She waited to see if he needed help, then continued. "I thought I knew everything about being a cop. The rules were black and white, right or wrong. Of course, now I know that there are no clear-cut rules. Everything is a different shade of gray."

"Do you like what you do?"

"It's ninety-ten, I suppose. Ninety percent is pure unbelievable crap, and ten percent is a smaller pile of crap. But I find it interesting." She hadn't thought about it for a while. There didn't seem to be a lot of extra time for wool-gathering, as her mother would have called it.

He thought about what she said. "True for me, too. Unfortunately, as a funeral director, people have to experience the loss of a friend or family member in order for me to get to know them. I try my best to be there for them, anticipate their needs, and be available to listen." Ella thought it wasn't far removed from being a policeman. "As a mortician, I try to understand what the family would like to see, or not see, during the service."

She understood what he was saying. "There is definitely a lot more to being a funeral director than I have considered, with my very inadequate knowledge on the subject. Thanks for telling me about it." She gave him a thumbs up, and smiled. "I don't normally share my personal life, like I've done with you," she admitted. "But, I feel comfortable here." His presence was calming, genuine. He was a good listener. *They are hard to find,* she thought. *Sometimes I don't think anybody listens to me.*

She lifted her glass to take a drink, only to find it empty. The ice in the pitcher had melted, too. *Time to go.* "I've really enjoyed talking with you, but I suppose I should be on my way." She didn't want to leave. She put her Cubs cap back on, and pulled her hair through the hole in the back. Her sunglasses rested on the top of her hat.

He seemed disappointed for a moment, then remembering something, stood up. "I completely forgot about Walter."

"Walter?"

"I'll be right back." He left by the kitchen door. She was puzzled. Who was Walter?

And then he returned, preceded by a large white-and-black dog with very short legs, long brown ears that grazed the floor, and a really big voice. He charged ahead, howling loudly, and ran to Ella like she was an old friend. He put his big, front feet on her legs and his snout in her face. Then, he threw his head back and howled again. "Walter?"

Jackson Lee was smiling at them. "Along with his house, your father left you his dog. A Bassett Hound named Walter."

Walter was quite a dog. She petted his silky ears and patted his head. Thankfully, it made him stop howling. She stroked his back. His coat was soft, and she came away with a handful of tiny hairs that she wiped on her pants. "He's very loud and he smells bad." Walter was panting, a string of slime hanging from his mouth. She used his ear to wipe it off. He stared at her with chestnut-colored eyes, love, and devotion.

"I know, but you get used to it." He was pleading with her.

"I'm sorry," she said, shaking her head. "No, I can't have a dog, I'm never home." There was no place for him in her busy life. "I'm always at work, or sleeping, or at Court, or the range."

"He doesn't take up much room," he argued. "He's a real social guy."

"I've never had a dog," she admitted. "That's a big responsibility."

"I won't argue with that. He's high maintenance." Walter glanced at them both, and Jackson Lee looked at her.

"Oh, crap," she conceded. "All right. He can come with me and stay the night at my father's house, but I'll have to leave him here when I go back to Chicago tomorrow."

"That's fair," he said. "He misses him so much." He picked up Walter's leash that was attached to a harness around his big body. "Here he is. I suppose all you need now are the keys to your father's house." He placed them in her hand along with the leash as they walked toward the side door, Walter plodding beside them.

"Thanks. I'll drop Walter off tomorrow on my way out of town." She wished she could stay longer, she really enjoyed his company. "Where's the house? I'll go there after I stop in at the police station."

"Important information," he said, chuckling to himself. "Follow the sidewalk in front of the funeral home like you're leaving town. The police station will be two blocks down on your left. It's on School Street and Main. Go down School Street a couple of blocks and you'll see a blue bungalow on the right. That's it."

He smiled, and bent down to kiss her cheek. "It's been a pleasure meeting you." As an afterthought, he said: "By the way, is there a Mr. Ella?"

When his lips brushed her skin, she became light-headed for a second. She smiled and answered, "No. No Mr. Ella." He liked her, she could tell.

Jackson Lee opened the door for the two of them. Ella was smiling to herself as they left, Yes, she really liked him, too. Too bad she was leaving tomorrow.

Hot air rushed in from the street to remind her of the hot, summer day. She could see dark clouds moving in from the west, so rain was on the way. Maybe it would cool things down. Walter led the way out.

Chapter 4
The Prosper Police Department
Tuesday Afternoon

The town of Prosper was a big departure from the city of Chicago. A sign Ella passed on the way into town estimated the population at 2,500 people, minus the recently departed Ray Flynn, of course. So, 2,499 people.

Ella and Walter ambled their way to the Police Department two blocks away. On her right, they came upon a large community park with a Civil War cannon, positioned on top of a raised concrete slab. It was located under an enormous Live Oak tree. Shaded by the tree, too, was a gazebo painted red, white, and blue. She could almost hear band music and feel the breeze that would flutter the two-story flag as it stood alongside the hundred-year-old tree. It could have been a postcard.

Across the street, and in front of the hardware store, sat two older, black gentlemen in rocking chairs. She named them Mr. Long Legs and Mr. Whittle. Mr. Long Legs rocked really slow, and Mr. Whittle was probably never seen without a knife and piece of wood. He sat bent over and sullen, whittling.

They both stopped rocking in favor of studying her. She waved and smiled, and got a chin jut of recognition in return. She lightly pulled the leash to attract Walter's attention, and waved goodbye as they continued slowly down the sidewalk.

Walter was an interesting dog, Ella thought. He had a penchant for examining dead and smelly things. He had sniffed out a decomposing bird next to the sidewalk and acted like he was going to perform an internal exam. "Not today, Walter," she said, pulling lightly on his leash. He glanced at her, then resumed his investigation. When he decided he was done, they moved on.

On the corner of Main Street and School Street, a two-story brick building with a cornerstone marked 1901, monopolized the corner. First National Bank was engraved in brick on the very top. At some point in time, the bank had become the Police Department.

A Prosper police car was parked in front of the building, along with a Harley-Davidson Fat Boy motorcycle with a sheepskin seat liner. "Ooh, baby," she said, patting the soft sheepskin. "I wish you were mine." Walter raised his leg to pee on it, but she stopped him. "That's a felony, buddy."

She pushed the door marked "pull," then tried the other one. Walter followed her inside. He sniffed around until he found a place he liked, turned around three times, and dropped his ass in the corner.

The interior still resembled a bank from the early 1900s, with very high ceilings and ornate architectural details. In contrast, heavy steel desks from the 1960s populated the large room. Ceiling fans hung from the rafters, listlessly spinning the warm air.

She counted eight desks, along with several offices in the back. Desk Number One was the closest to the door, and empty. If necessary, she would be able to recall the inside of the police department in minute detail.

Desk Number Two faced the side windows. It was occupied by a female police officer, who glanced up and smiled at her.

Ella smiled back. "Hi," she said. "I'm Detective Ella Flynn from Chicago." She showed her the Chicago star in her wallet.

The officer nodded her head in approval and walked over to

extend her hand. "Officer Consuelo Lopez. You can call me Connie. Pleased to meet you, Detective."

Connie was a big girl. She wore a midnight blue short-sleeved uniform, with darker blue trousers. Her hair was quite short and curly, bleached snowy white. It showed off her tawny skin. "Your little friend down there looks familiar," she said, gesturing to Walter.

Ella looked down. "Yes, a parting gift from my recently deceased father." She liked Connie. "Walter and I just met." She continued. "I'm in town because my father, Ray Flynn, died yesterday and I needed to finalize a few things at the funeral home. I just wanted to stop in and introduce myself." Officer Connie nodded in acknowledgement.

"We were expecting you. Your father had a newspaper clipping of you at a Chicago Police Department ceremony, or we would never have been able to find you."

"Yes, I found that out from Jackson Lee, at the Armstrong Funeral Home." She was very pleased with that discovery.

"Oh, good," she said. "You've already met with him." Then she added: "We're sorry about your loss, Detective." Officer Connie looked appropriately sad. "If there's any way we can be of assistance, let us know."

It probably wasn't heart-felt, but it made her feel better. "Thank you. Also, I thought I'd say hey to the Chief while I was in town. Is he or she available?"

"Chief Lovey Jones is expected shortly, if you'd like to wait." She pointed to a chair by the wall. Ella promptly sat down. She took off her Cubs hat and rested it on her knee, then slid her sunglasses to the top of her head and wiped the sweat from her forehead with the back of her hand. It wasn't much cooler inside than it was outside.

Minutes later, the door to her left dinged as it opened.

The man who entered reminded her of a Chicago Bears fullback. Powerful, tall and broad, with the same type of blue shirt and pants as Officer Connie, but they looked very different on him. He had a regulation cop mustache that resembled a UPC code, and a rich, dark umber complexion. Ella quickly stood up, accidentally dropping her Cubs hat on the floor. She grabbed it, then stuck out her right hand and said: "Detective Ella Flynn from the Chicago Police Department, Sir."

He grabbed her hand in his paw and visibly shook it up and down. "Nice to meet you, Detective Flynn. I'm Chief Lovey Jones." His voice was very deep and soft around the edges. "We don't often get visitors from the big city of Chicago. This here is Sergeant Nightengale," the Chief said, pointing to the man who followed him through the door. "You can call him Bobby Dean. Everybody does."

Sergeant Bobby Dean was very young, pale, and gaunt. Without a belt, his pants would have pooled on the floor. She stuck her hand out again. The young man hesitated, then shook it. His hand was cold and bony, like a bag of marbles. His eyes were evasive. He reminded her of a fledging bird, anxious and unsure. *Strange qualities for a police officer*, she thought. He took his hand back as soon as he could.

"Sorry about the weather here. Hotter than the hinges of hell out there today. Storms coming tonight though. Thanks for coming," the Chief said in a monotone, stringing all the words together. "First, we're very sorry for your loss. Ray was a valued member of the community and we'll miss him." He smiled down at her.

She smiled back. "Thank you. Please call me Ella," she said. "I just wanted to introduce myself and tell you I'm in town. I'll leave my card with you," she said, handing it to him. "It has my cell phone number on the back in case you need to reach me."

He moved a little closer to her. Just enough to make her uncomfortable, about one foot into her comfort zone. "I appreciate that, detective," he said. "How long do you plan to be in Prosper?" His eyes were very dark, and she couldn't read them.

She awkwardly took a step back. "I just met with the funeral director down the street. He gave me the dog," she said, pointing to Walter by her feet. "I'm giving him back when I leave tomorrow morning. Just gonna wait for the autopsy results, then fly back to Chicago."

Chief Jones rubbed his chin with the knuckles on his right hand. "Yeah, the autopsy. I didn't expect that. Looks like a heart attack to me. What about you, Bobby Dean?"

He had been cleaning his fingernails with a key and looked startled. "What?"

"Heart attack. Looks like a heart attack." The Chief seemed irritated.

"Oh, yeah, Chief," Bobby Dean agreed, nodding his head. "It was a heart attack for sure."

Ella nodded her head, too. "All right then. I guess it was a heart attack. They'll confirm it tomorrow and I'll be back in Chicago tomorrow afternoon. Tonight, me and Walter are gonna stay at my father's house down the street." She didn't think they cared about where she slept, but said it anyway.

"If you've got a minute, let's go back to my office and get to know each other." The Chief didn't wait for her response, quickly walking off with Sgt. Bobby Dean. She grabbed Walter's leash and followed them into the room. He closed the door.

The office wasn't big, but it had a nice desk that the Chief sat behind, and a few chairs, currently occupied by Sgt. Bobby Dean and her. Walter appraised the situation and located a shady spot under the desk for a nap.

"So, you're a big city cop, Flynn." He smiled, and rocked back in his chair. "We're hearing all the time down here about crime in Chicago, everybody shooting everybody else. Is that right?"

She couldn't deny it. "Big gang problems. Drive-by shootings. Murder. Death. General mayhem." She smiled back.

The Chief chuckled. Sgt. Bobby Dean sat in the corner, arms crossed, a smirk on his skinny face. "I like you, Flynn," he said. "What do you do there?"

She repeated what she told Jackson Lee about her involvement with the Violent Crimes Unit and the type of crimes they worked on. If possible, she was even more vague. "We are way overloaded. My Chief only gave me two days' leave, but I'm pretty sure I'll only need one. I'll make a speedy exit." She smiled. He was a very personable man, and she liked him, too.

"Sorry you're going back right away. I understand, though. We're a little understaffed right now and days off are limited, aren't they, Bobby Dean?"

He looked like his mind had been wandering and the school teacher just asked him a question. "What?"

The Chief's eyes squinted when he glared at him. "We're having a conversation here. Are you aware of that?"

"Yes, sir," he said, sitting up straight.

"Pay. Attention." The Chief didn't look angry, but his words were clipped and direct.

"Yes, sir," he said, again.

The Chief looked back at Ella. "Have you been to Prosper before to visit your father?" A reasonable question.

"I have not," she said, with a smile. "I haven't seen my father since I was seven years old. He drove away, and never came back." It was a fact, not a big deal. "My mom told me he went back to his hometown in Georgia."

He frowned. "Why do you suppose he did that? Just up and left his family?" He seemed genuinely concerned.

It was a very personal question from someone she just met, but she didn't mind talking about it. He seemed empathetic. "Thinking back, there were signs, I guess." She crossed her legs. "My mom was a nurse and wasn't home much. When she was home, he was drunk. I don't think she was a fan of that. I remember he lost his job and was out of work for quite a while. I liked that part, because he was always around to play with me." She smiled.

The Chief nodded his head. "I see that a lot in domestic disturbances around here. Alcohol, poverty, no jobs. Like dry wood set on fire." *He understood*, she thought.

"He had a few reasons to leave. I can see that," she admitted. "But the part I have never understood is why he never contacted me. He knew where I lived." When she frowned, the lines around her mouth deepened.

The Chief looked directly at her. "You knew he was here. Why didn't you contact him?"

That stung. She glanced away from him. "No, he had to make the first move because he left me." On this point, she was adamant.

"Ella, look at me," he said. She did. "Life isn't a game. People aren't chess pieces, and nobody waits for his turn. I feel kinda bad saying this to you, but you have to own your part in this problem." His face was kind, even if she didn't like what he said.

She was a little angry, and sat up. She crossed her arms in front of her. "What do you mean?" Her lips were set in a tight, thin line.

The Chief smiled. "Don't be mad. I'm just saying this street goes two ways. You could have contacted him. You could have yelled at him and asked him why he left. You could have forgiven him and come to visit. The thing is, you chose not to." His voice had softened.

Ella sat very still, on the edge of tears. "I think this conversation is over." She stood up, and tightened the leash to get Walter's attention. "Thank you for your time." She nodded to Sgt. Bobby Dean. Walter padded out of the office, and she closed the door behind her.

Officer Connie smiled. "Well, that was quick."

Ella didn't return her smile. "Does he meddle in everybody's life?" She was still stinging from the Chief's advice. *He doesn't even know me.*

She laughed. "He grabs on like an alligator."

"Mind if I sit here a minute and check my messages?"

"That's just fine. Take your time." When Connie handed her a bottle of water and offered her a desk to sit at, Ella gratefully took up residence. She slid her phone out of her pocket and scrolled through her emails. They were steadily accumulating. Her attention was quickly diverted to four urgent answer-right-now texts and two missed phone calls. A notification gave her the news that the Chicago Cubs lost 13 to 4 to Milwaukee. *My kingdom for a relief pitcher*, she thought. She made short work of the texts and answered the phone calls. She was unable to do anything about the Cubs and their slack offense.

"So, you're a Chicago detective," Connie said, dragging a chair next to the desk. She had a very pleasant personality that invited conversation, and Ella was genuinely interested in the small-town police department.

"Guilty," she answered, laying her phone on the desk, and turning to face her.

"What's it like? A lot busier than here, I'm sure." Connie's brown eyes were wide open.

"It's a big city, all right," she answered. "More than eight million people, I think." *Chicago and Prosper might as well be in different universes*, she thought.

"Do tell. We're a pretty small town." She laughed out loud. "I suppose you noticed that. What type of work do you do there?"

"I work Area One. I'm a detective." She was proud of her job, and it came across.

Connie seemed impressed, and a little skeptical. She ran her fingers through her soft, clipped hair. "I don't imagine I'd like such a big city. I think this little town is more than enough for me."

Ella checked out the small office. "This is different. Definitely." She glanced at the clock. The afternoon was moving by quickly. "What do you guys have going on?"

The Chief wandered back into the office in time to hear her question. "We're mighty busy here, matter of fact. Last night we had a drug deal gone bad at the Super Eight Motel. One man shot. He's at the hospital in Jessup."

She wasn't surprised the small-town façade hid some violence. "Is that unusual?"

He considered the question. "I wish it was, but no, it isn't. Last week, a man down by the river, that's the Altamaha River I'm talking about, smacked his wife around until she beat him to death with a cast-iron skillet."

She smiled. "Glad I missed that one."

"Wish I had. Messy." He looked nauseated for a minute. "Sex trafficking is a big threat in the South, and I guess everywhere else, too. We help the Georgia Bureau of Investigation out as much as we can, but we're a pretty small department. Drinking, drugs, shootings. I'm sure you know what it's like."

Connie broke in. "Trouble is, we're a little short-handed. Calvin, he works weekends, fell off his roof trying to lay shingles and broke his leg. Bobby Dean here," she said, pointing to the young man sitting at a desk in the back, "why he's been working seven days straight. I don't know how he does it."

Bobby Dean gave the group a disinterested look, then went back to his phone.

"Right now, we're following up on a few leads about a residential burglary Sunday night" the Chief added. "And, of course, processing the death of your father. Besides all the usual crap that takes place every day."

Ella watched her phone vibrate on the desk. "Yeah, I know just what you mean." She glanced at the clock again.

She slid her phone into the front pocket of her pants, wound her hair through the hole in the rear of her Cubs hat and set the cap in place. "By the way, where's a good place to eat in this town?" There needed to be a restaurant in her near future.

"The Sunshine Café is open all day," Connie answered. "It's about a block down the street. Their food is mighty tasty. And there's a bait shop called 'The Worm Ranch' by the river. Don't eat there unless you're drunk."

"Good information." she mentally crossed The Worm Ranch off her list. "I guess we'll drop by my father's house before supper." She stood up, then bent over to pull her khaki's down over her ankle holster.

"Really nice meeting you," Connie said. The Chief gave her a wave. Ella waved back.

She put on her sunglasses. *This trip can't get over soon enough*, she thought. She lightly tugged Walter off the floor and directed him to the door. They would have to return to the Armstrong Funeral Home to pick up the car, and drive to her father's blue house.

Chapter 5
The Blue House
Tuesday Afternoon

Ella thought the house was hideous, at least from the outside. There must have been a sale on blue paint because everything, including the shutters, was painted blue. The door was blue. The porch was blue. The blue paint was peeling off the house, the blue wooden porch was spongy and rotten, and the blue window frames needed to be replaced. *Egads*, Ella thought.

She parked the car on the street and the dog quickly slid out of the front seat. Walter waddled down the sidewalk, black tail with a white tip, straight up and batting the air. He was very strong, a large-sized dog, but with very short legs. He bounded up the four stairs, and sat expectantly in front of the door, eager to go in. The key fit in the lock, but it didn't turn. It slid in and out. Finally, she put the key in and shook the handle up and down. It turned, and they were inside.

The small front room was stuffed with utilitarian furniture arranged on worn wood floors, with a tattered area rug to pull it all together. There was a wide TV in the corner, sitting on top of a smaller console TV that probably stopped working a decade or two ago. Ella pictured her father watching television with Walter curled up next to him. She wondered if they watched the same programs she did.

The dog had already taken up residence on the cigar-colored leather sofa. It was held together with varying colors of duct tape, covered with several small shabby blankets and throws. It was definitely broken in, and looked cozy and comfy to her, and obviously to Walter, too. She figured her father's body had been found on it.

An intricately made oak side-table with porcelain inlays and delicate features resided next to the sofa. Ray, the woodworker, must have made it. This was obviously not a genetic trait; her creativity level was below zero. Several wood-working magazines were stacked neatly under a lamp.

She did a quick survey of the house. The kitchen had an avocado-green refrigerator and stove from the 1970s. The dishes were washed and the floor wasn't sticky. Lying in the sink was an empty vodka bottle. The window over the sink showed a fenced backyard, big enough for a Bassett hound to chase squirrels and take a leisurely dump. It was adequate, and certainly big enough for her. If she decided to keep it, which she didn't think she would.

Mail was strewn across the undersized kitchen table. A bill from the city for water and garbage. An electric bill. The charges appeared to be up-to-date. Her father must have made enough money as a woodworker to pay his bills, this was good to know.

There were two bedrooms. One had a bed in it made up with sheets, a soft grey blanket, and a quilted bedspread. The sides were tucked in so tightly on the bed, a quarter would have bounced on it. She knew her father had served in the military by the precision of his bedmaking ability. The second bedroom seemed to have been used for storage. Magazines spilled out of boxes and books were stacked against the wall. Fishing equipment was strewn throughout. She had to stop Walter from snorting a treble hook.

The bathroom contained a bathtub with a shower head, regular toilet, and a sink with two spigots. The shower curtain was plastic with dingy yellow suns on it. She checked the hot and cold water. Everything worked.

Walter started whining about being hungry. She rummaged through the kitchen cabinets and was rewarded with small dry nuggets marketed as dog food, and a few cans of "meat with gravy and rice." He would think she was the greatest cook in the world. Lastly, she discovered a cold beer for herself.

After he ate, Walter slurped down a bowl of water, immediately converted it into urine, and went outside. Twice. He howled at something, barked, and performed a thorough inspection of the yard. A squirrel sat on the fence, patiently waiting for him to notice, then raced off. He howled in despair, then gave up the chase to return to the house.

Ella sat on the very comfortable sofa, sipping her beer. Reflecting on the day. Walter curled up next to her, full of dog food, and dozed off with his head in her lap. She stroked his long ears, removing pieces of his supper from the bottom ear parts that sat in the bowl while he ate.

She hadn't thought of her father for years, and now that he had died, she could think of little else. He probably pushed her on a swing or read to her on the sofa. They could have been happy. She just didn't know. What she did remember, was the bang of the kitchen screen door and the crunch of gravel as his car backed down the driveway for the last time.

The heady aroma of beer reminded her of him. He always gave her the first sip. The odor of gasoline evoked images of his hands, fingernails stained with oil from the gas station where he worked.

Ella had spent years consciously trying to erase him from her mind. And then yesterday, when hit with his death, she was reminded that he had still existed in Georgia.

Her mother, Susan, a self-described recovering romantic, insisted the two of them were star-crossed lovers. She told Ella how they met when she was studying to be a nurse and waitressing nights at a diner on Rush Street in Chicago. Her father had recently moved from Georgia to

Chicago following a three-year stint in the army.

Every day, around supper time, he came into the diner where her mother worked. She said he sat at the same table in the corner and read a book. Every night, her mother told her, she talked to him whether he liked it or not. She flirted. He was unenthusiastic. She pried. He parried. The more he resisted, the harder she tried.

She finally wore him down. She knew he was flawed, but he ignited the need in her to nurse him to happiness. Her mother was naïve. She didn't understand that you can't change people. No matter how hard you try.

Her father gave in and they were married at the County Clerk's office in Chicago seven months before Ella was born. They rented a small house in the city and he found a job at a neighborhood gas station pumping gas and fixing cars. Her mother finished her nursing degree just before Ella arrived. In the nick of time, she always told her, with a smile.

When Ella's father left them, life went on. Her mother struggled with the loss of her husband, grieving for a long time, but consumed with the job of taking care of Ella. Her neighborhood in Wicker Park was overwhelmed with children of every age and size. She had everything she wanted, except a father. Her mother never married again. But it was okay, Ella thought, the two of them did just fine. When her mother was diagnosed with breast cancer, she was the caregiver, cheerleader, and advocate. Her mother died last year.

Yesterday, Ella's father died. She had never felt more alone.

Chapter 6
The Sunshine Café
Tuesday night

The Sunshine Café was teeming with local townsfolk feasting on the Tuesday night fried chicken special, when Ella walked in. Sitting alone in a booth across the room, she saw Officer Connie Lopez. She waved off the hostess and presented herself, hoping to join her. Connie looked up from the menu she held, and smiled.

"Well, look who's here," she said, motioning for her to sit down. "You'll make my supper a little more interesting." Ella slid into the booth across from her.

"Thanks, Connie. I wasn't looking forward to eating alone." Connie had changed into black pants, a white t-shirt, and a black leather vest. In addition to a number of patches, the emblem on the vest read "Hillbilly Bastards."

"Where's the dog?" Connie asked, looking around.

"My little friend, Walter. Turns out, he goes to bed early. He made a little nest on the rug in the bathroom and closed the door behind him." He definitely looked like he was out for the night.

"Not terribly convenient for you." Connie was matter-of-fact about it. She didn't mince words.

"It's only one night. I'll deal with it. I noticed a Harley Fat Boy in the parking lot. Yours?"

"That's my baby." She smiled a very big smile.

"And your bike club is the Hillbilly Bastards?"

"That's right," she said, proudly. With the change in clothes, the metamorphosis from police officer to biker bitch was complete.

Ella was familiar with motorcycle clubs in Chicago. Much different than illicit motorcycle gangs. The clubs were usually composed of people with similar interests, including motorcycles, of course. Connie looked pretty tame, although she could be wrong.

She searched the area for a waitress. "I'm so hungry I could eat the left side of the menu." Her stomach was screaming.

"Relax," Connie said. "The fried chicken comes with macaroni and cheese, fried okra, collard greens, cornbread, and pecan pie." Obviously, this wasn't her first fried chicken supper at the Sunshine Café.

Pen in hand, a young woman stopped to take their order. Her name plate revealed her name was Stella.

"Marlene makes the best fried chicken in Georgia," Connie said. Stella nodded her head in agreement.

"Best damn chicken," Stella reiterated. "Whattaya want, Sweetie?" She was chewing gum like it was a contest, and she was winning.

"We want two of them fried chicken specials."

Stella didn't write it down. "What're you drinking?"

Ella was dying for a cold beer.

"Same here," Connie said.

In what seemed like mere seconds, the beer and food appeared. Plates filled the table. Knives and forks clanked and scraped. Conversation was held to mutters and exclamations of joy. Over time, the population of diners dwindled. When the pecan pie arrived, the din in the diner had decreased, talking was easier.

Connie wiped her hands on a napkin. "So, what're you working on?"

Ella took a moment to think about it. "There were fifty-four shootings in Chicago last weekend, so we're pretty busy."

She seemed very interested. "Damn. I bet you see a lot of action."

Ella had been well-schooled on not sharing information about her police work with the public, so she changed the subject. "I'm sure you have some interesting cases, too."

She gazed out the window. "No," she said, chewing on her lower lip. "Occasional domestic violence maybe. We had a lady the other day steal a Shop & Save scooter to drive to the post office."

Ella chuckled. This was the kind of case she liked. Crazy people doing silly things. Not gang-on-gang drive-by shootings where innocent people were killed. Telling a mother her son was collateral damage. You never get over that.

"Why'd you decide to be a cop?" she asked Connie. Ella was always interested in why police officers chose this particular career.

"I guess it was when my aunt was murdered about ten years ago." She didn't look at Ella. "The guy who did it had just got outta prison for killing his grandma. He only got three years for that." She smiled in Ella's direction. "I guess that's more of a misdemeanor."

Ella shook her head. "That's awful. Do you know why he did it?"

Connie smiled a sardonic smile. "He drove her to the bank first, to get some money to buy his girlfriend a ring. So, there's that. Then drove her back home and killed her." She paused. "Why did he do it? Because he enjoyed it." She still seemed angry.

"Yes, I know these people exist," Ella assured her. "I'm so sorry about your aunt. That's a terrible loss."

"At least he's locked up now. I wish I'd caught the bastard." She was distracted, chewing on a fingernail.

"So that made you want to be a cop?" It was certainly enough.

Connie put her hands on the table and evaluated her fingernails.

"Time for a manicure," she said, and looked at Ella. "Yeah, that, along with all the rest of the crime here. I remember wanting to make a difference. What about you?"

Ella thought about it. "I spent my entire childhood wanting to be a cop. It's the way I've always seen myself."

Connie appeared to be deep in thought. "Being a woman, how are you treated in Chicago?"

Ella rubbed her temples with the tips of her fingers. She had a headache. "Most of the men are fine with me and treat me like one of the guys. But, there's a segment that resent my presence." *They make it obvious by leaving me out, not passing on important information,* she thought. "They don't trust me. Don't trust that when they need me, I'll step up. That I've got their back no matter what happens."

"I get that."

"I've been with the Chicago PD for eight years. If they don't know me by now and trust me, I can't do anything to change their minds." It was frustrating. Ella wished she knew how to gain their confidence.

Connie was quiet. "I might be better off in Prosper. I've got a big mouth and that gets me in lots of trouble. Lucky for me, the Chief likes me."

Ella squirmed in her seat. "He got really personal with me a little while ago. Too personal. I don't like that. My Chief in Chicago is a sullen, miserable son-of-a-bitch who doesn't even know I have a personal life." She smiled at Connie. "I think I prefer that."

"The Chief likes to fix people, whether they want to be fixed or not. What did he say?"

She studied her bottle of beer. "He asked why my father left my mom and me when I was a little girl." Connie looked surprised.

"I didn't know your father did that. Did he ever tell you why?"

"I haven't spoken with him since he left more than twenty years ago."

Connie shook her head, "My, my, my. What did you say to the Chief?"

"The truth. My mother was a nurse and worked a lot. My father was a drunk and drank a lot. He lost his job. He drove off into the sunset never to be heard from again. That sums it up." She waited for Connie's reaction.

"What's the part that made you so angry?"

Ella had been considering what he said for a while. "He told me if I wanted to reach out to my father, I knew where he was, and I could have contacted him any time I wanted."

"Oh." Connie nodded in agreement. "I guess that's true."

"It is true." Ella glanced in her direction. "That's the part that makes me so angry. I wish I could go back and change things, but I can't. I'm angry at myself," she admitted. She decided to keep the lesson in the file marked 'being an adult' in her head.

"He means well, Chief Lovey Jones." She rearranged the salt and pepper shakers. "He's been here for about four years. Appointed by the Mayor. Married, and his wife has Parkinson's, so he spends a lot of his time taking care of her."

Ella put the salt and pepper shakers back in their little house.

Connie put her hands together to admire her teal-colored fingernails. "He has a gruff exterior, but inside is mush."

"How does he treat you?"

"Like he's my dad," she laughed. "No, I'm just kidding. He's very respectful, and I like him a lot." Connie smiled. "I guess I do what he expects of me, or maybe a little more."

"I like that," Ella said. "Chief Warner keeps me at a distance, like everybody else. He's not a warm and fuzzy guy."

Connie made a steeple of her fingers. "Have you met the Mayor yet?"

"No, I haven't. Should I?"

"Mayor Big Dick Wheeler rules the roost. He thinks he's the king of Prosper." Connie frowned. "He's an ass."

"Excuse me," Ella said, stopping her. "His name is Big Dick?"

Connie lowered her voice to a hoarse whisper. "It has been said that Big Dick got his nickname after he was caught screwing the lunch lady in the back seat of his car in the Waffle House parking lot." Connie winked.

"Seriously?" Ella laughed.

"If it isn't true, it should be." Connie puckered her lips. "As long as I've been around, everybody calls him that. Before he was Mayor, he was Big Dick Wheeler. Now he's Mayor Big Dick Wheeler."

Ella giggled. "I'm sorry. I can't call him that. I'll just call him Mayor."

"Well, then you'll love this. His son is Little Dick Wheeler, but goes by Junior. Daughter's named Princess."

"Wow. What's his wife's name?"

"Maud. She runs the Historical Society Museum in Jessup."

And then, like it was preordained, the Mayor and his family filed into the restaurant. Ella switched seats with Connie to take a good look at them. The father was shaped like an egg with a belt around the biggest part of his belly.

He placed himself at the head of the rectangular table, Maud to his right and Princess to his left. Son, Junior, sat at the other end with a dissatisfied look on his face. The Mayor talked on his phone, and Princess had her head down scrolling on hers. Maud glanced around at the people in the restaurant and her lips smiled, but the rest of her face didn't. Junior answered his phone, then stood up and walked out the door.

The Mayor ignored it and ordered his supper from Stella, still working on her gum. He continued with his phone call. Maud and Princess ordered next.

"Strange family dynamic," Ella noted. "Are they always like this?"

"Pretty much," Connie confirmed.

They asked for another beer, and sat in silence for a while. "What can you tell me about Bobby Dean?" Ella asked. He seemed so disinterested in what was going on when she met him.

Connie seemed thoughtful. "He's not a bad guy, but he has a lot of issues. He follows the Chief around like he's attached to him. I think the Chief feels sorry for him because he's had a pretty shitty life, so he lets him tag along. He was a foster kid, tossed around for years in the system before Father Santos got him."

"Father Santos?"

"The Catholic Priest at the funny-looking church on the way out of town."

"What do you mean 'funny looking?'"

"It was built with the roof flat in the center, with the sides going up. We call it 'the church that God sat on.'"

She chuckled and nodded her head. "Okay, he takes in foster kids?"

"He used to, but I don't think he does anymore. My partner was a foster kid, too, and ended up living with Father Santos."

"It sounds like he's a great guy for being a foster parent," she said, wanting to know the truth.

"You'd think so, wouldn't you?" Connie looked like she had a secret.

"He's not so great?"

"He'd like you to believe he's charming as hell. But that's a disguise. I've heard he can be a real bastard. Dixie has told me some awful stories about living there. If you want to know more about Bobby Dean, you should talk to her."

Ella shook her head. "I'll remember that, but I doubt if I will. Leaving tomorrow after all."

"If you change your mind, Dixie is always at our house on School Street. We're rehabbing a house we bought at auction," she looked proud. "It's a real piece of shit but we're making headway. We've got a working bathroom." Connie seemed to radiate happiness at this fact. "She's a surgeon with power tools."

Ella laughed. "A working bathroom is definitely on my "must have" list.

The restaurant had cleared out, but they both had a fresh beer demanding to be consumed. Connie wasn't finished talking, anyway. "There's a lot about Prosper you should know. For instance, this little town was named after Captain Luscious T. Prosper of the Fourth Brigade, Georgia Militia, who held the Altamaha Trestle Bridge during the Civil War. They prevented General Sherman's troops from passing through."

"Captain Prosper." Ella smiled.

"Known by his troops as Captain Never Prosper, he was drunk and incontinent at the time of the skirmish. You can read all about it on a plaque by the Civil War cannon in the park."

"It really says he was drunk?" She was fascinated.

"Maybe not. I could have made that part up." Connie enjoyed gossiping about the little town and its people, fact or fiction.

"What can you tell me about Jackson Lee, the funeral director I met today?"

She smiled. "I like him. He's my bingo partner Friday nights at the Catholic Church."

"Has he got a girlfriend?" Ella hated to ask.

"I've seen women come and go," Connie said. "He went off to college for a while, but came back to run the funeral home when his father died. I can tell you he's a fantastic cook."

"He is?" She was surprised. None of the men she knew enjoyed cooking.

"He loves to host supper parties to show off his skills, and I've been to a few of them." She smiled. "I sure hope he invites me again."

"He's really interesting, isn't he?" she asked Connie, who was rearranging the condiments on the table.

"You like him, don't you?" She had a sly smile.

"I guess I do," Ella said.

"What about you, girl?"

It was Ella's turn to rearrange the condiments. "I've got a guy back home," she admitted.

"That's nice, isn't it?"

She shook her head. "Not really. It's like a one-night stand that just won't end. He wants me to move in with him. I'd like to move farther away from him." She added: "Dating someone you work with is a big mistake."

"Fellow policeman?" Connie asked, smiling.

"I knew it was a bad idea, and did it anyway." *I don't know what I was thinking,* she thought. *If I break up with him, everybody in the police department will hate me.*

"Ah, paradise."

"I just can't find the right guy, I've always got one foot out the door so I can leave him before he leaves me," she admitted. She didn't trust him. It wasn't his fault; he was up against years of bad choices on her part.

"Relationships aren't easy. I've been with Dixie for about five years now. I love her like crazy, but we're two very different people. She's neat, I'm not. She's the power tool queen, I'm not. She's a great cook, I'm not. But we both love motorcycles, and that's our connection." Connie pursed her lips in thought. "Living with somebody is a bitch sometimes," she said.

"You know it is," Ella agreed. She sucked the last little bit of beer from the bottle. "I guess I should get on home. It's been a very informative evening, Connie."

She nodded her head in agreement.

"I enjoyed talking with you and learning about Captain Never Prosper." She was suddenly exhausted. "I'll see you tomorrow, after I drop Walter off at the funeral home."

Connie waved goodbye.

The air outside the restaurant was heavy, damp, and explosive. The wind had whipped up a breeze that turned the leaves upside down in the trees. Ella walked quickly down the street to the blue house. Just as she closed the door behind her, hard rain hit the sidewalk.

Walter howled from the bathroom. He could close the door behind him, but he couldn't open it. Just not tall enough. When Ella let him out, he continued howling, not once, but over and over. She wasn't sure if he was glad she was home, or pissed that she had left. Hard to tell.

When she finally lay down on the sofa, he hopped up and curled up next to her with his head on her legs. He smelled like Fritos, the Fritos you find on the floor in the backseat of your car. She'll get used to it. Right.

Longest day. Ever.

Chapter 7
Mayor Big Dick Wheeler
Wednesday Morning

The Office of the Mayor

Mayor Big Dick Wheeler was in the office early Wednesday morning, which, along with the Commerce Commission, was located on the second floor of the old bank building, above the police department. He stared out the window at the street below, already dry after the storm, and not a cloud in the sky. The Coroner from Jessup parked his Honda Civic on the street, and went into the building. He knew the Medical Examiner from the Georgia Bureau of Investigation was already inside.

This meeting was about the autopsy results on Ray Flynn. They didn't usually get a visit by the M.E. from Savannah. He didn't like it. It made him nervous.

He inserted his thumbs inside his belt while he was looking out the window, and reflected on his current problem, his son, Junior. The boy wouldn't listen. When he told him to stay away from that girl, what did he do? He went out with her. She's trouble, he told his son. It wouldn't end well. But the boy just doesn't listen.

He checked his messages. Everybody was to meet downstairs at ten o'clock, an hour from now. He sent a message to Junior to tell him to be there. The kid was only twenty, but he wanted him in the Police Department, and he would force Chief Jones to take him, if necessary.

He paced from window to window, finally sitting at his desk to check his emails. Papers were stacked in his inbox, many had been there for a year or more. Another, taller stack, to his left was a repository for all things related to his personal investments. It held the deeds for the hardware store, Levon Liquor Store, and a few houses in town. He kept this money a secret from Maud.

He took the cap off the bottle of antacids, and shoved two pills in his mouth. The kid had given him an ulcer. If he would have listened, all this could have been avoided. He had a bad feeling about the whole nasty thing, and his stomach was doing somersaults.

Chapter 8
Chief Lovey Jones
Wednesday morning

Chief Lovey Jones

Chief Lovey Jones was holed up in his office, alone, peering out on the scene before him. He could see the Medical Examiner from the Savannah office of the Georgia Bureau of Investigation lugging her big briefcase into the large conference room where he'd had Connie set up a bunch of chairs.

Bobby Dean was twitching like a bug, standing up, sitting down. Checking his phone. What the hell was wrong with him? He was trying so hard to make a man out of him. Sometimes it seemed like an impossibility. Connie was making coffee. Big Dick wasn't there yet.

For such a simple case as a heart attack, this was uncommon. He usually got a call from the GBI with the results of the autopsy, and that was what he had been expecting. When the M.E. from Savannah showed up this morning, he was very surprised. Loretta Mae Montgomery. She was all business. He'd met her once before at the lab in Savannah. Good looking woman.

Junior Wheeler sauntered in on his way to the conference room. Big Dick was pushing him to hire the kid, but he was dancing as fast as he could to avoid it. Kid was a smart ass. He hoped the Mayor would lose the next election before he had to make a decision.

The Mayor came in around quarter to ten. The only one left was Flynn. He'd called her about ten minutes ago. He sighed. He liked her. It really was too bad her father died before she could connect with him. He wished he could have helped.

Connie knocked on the glass and motioned for him to come out. He didn't want to come out, but he couldn't hide in his office behind a big see-through window, either. Might as well join the group.

Chapter 9
The Blue House
Wednesday Morning

Walter wasn't on the sofa with her when Ella woke up. With the first crack of thunder last night, he was off the sofa and headed to his master suite in the bathroom. She heard him close the door behind him with a click. Now he was whining to be set free. She would have to remember to keep the door closed so he couldn't lock himself in again.

When Ella opened the bathroom door, Walter headed for the back door. A squirrel taunted him from a tree, so naturally he began to howl, a very special treat for the neighbors who had planned to sleep in. After he deposited a pile that was visible from space, she let him back in.

The storms last night had been furious. Lacking any type of insulation between the house walls and the outside world, the wind threatened to blow the house away. The rain beat down on the roof until water steadily dripped in the middle of the room. Ella set up a bucket to catch the water, and it made the sound of the drips echo when they hit the bottom. It wasn't long before there was enough water in the pail to cushion the noise.

The storm didn't bother her, she was numb, and her sleep was dreamless. She woke up to loud and obnoxious bird tweets, even though it was still black outside. One single streetlight gave off a hazy glow. The air was already warm, but much less humid.

Ella set a small coffee pot on the gas stove and only had to try three burners before she found one that worked. She clumped ground coffee into the basket, and as soon as the water roiled and popped, she turned the flame down and waited the necessary five minutes for the liquid to change into a dark, aromatic brew. It smelled like hot tar. And just like that, the day was set in motion.

Together they watched the yellow sun slowly emerge from the dark horizon and change the sky from orange to blue.

Walter sat next to her on the sofa with his head on her lap. With each stroke on his back, she came away with a handful of little white hairs. She figured that in a short time, she would be able to knit herself another Bassett hound. A companion for Walter. His ears were wet from dragging in the grass after the storm, and she rubbed them dry. His eyes slowly rolled back in his head as he dozed off.

She hadn't been able to break the code with his facial expressions. It was hard to tell if he was happy, or really angry. She did know if there was a string of slime emanating from his jowls, he was hungry. With this knowledge, Walter was easy to get along with. He was her constant companion, and it was nice to have someone to talk to.

"Yesterday was so busy, Walter, it feels good to finally rest. Don't you agree?" He gazed up at her, then began to lick his right paw intently. "I'll tell you this in confidence, buddy. The police department down here doesn't feel right to me. There's a balance missing." She waited for the dog to respond, and when he didn't, she continued. "There aren't enough of them, for one thing. It's a good thing it's quiet around here." She took a long sip of her no-longer-hot coffee, and stared out the window. "And then there's Jackson Lee with the two first names. He's an interesting guy, all right." She put her cup on the floor next to the sofa. Walter seemed noncommittal. "You're such a good listener," she told him. He thumped his tail.

Ella had definitely warmed up to the dog. He had three different levels of communication. When he was talking to you or complaining about you, he yowled, over and over again at maximum volume. When he saw another dog or a person, or thought he saw someone, he barked, which was a WOW sound. When he wanted something from you, he whined like a toddler on a sugar high. If he was quiet, he was asleep.

Ella stood up, carefully moving the dog's head. "While we're waiting for the autopsy results, we might as well go through my father's stuff." Walter eagerly jumped off the sofa and followed her down the hall, toenails clacking on the floor.

Together they hit the bedroom with the bed in it, tossing clothes from the closet into piles on the floor. Several flannel shirts were wadded up on the closet floor along with a diverse array of shoes and boots. She added them to one of the piles, and gave a pair of ragged, stinky slippers to Walter for chewing. He seemed to enjoy the taste of feet.

In the second bedroom, she zeroed in on several cardboard boxes keeping each other company in the corner. The first box held a community of small bugs, fishing gear, lures, waders, and an astounding color array of plastic worms, from transparent brown to metallic emerald. She packed it back up and marked it with the words: Fishing Crap.

The second box was more interesting. Of consequence, it held several trophies her father had won, letters rubber-banded together, and papers from his time in the Army. The letters were from Ella's mother to him. She was surprised he kept them. It didn't fit in with the snarky image she gave him. Neither did his wallet with the newspaper article about her. The more she learned about him, the more convinced she became that she may have to alter her view.

The earliest of her mother's letters was light and charming, still smelling slightly of perfume, asking her father to visit her at the diner where she worked. Ella caught her breath when she saw her mother's handwriting. The ache in her heart was still fresh.

Subsequent letters became more insistent, asking him to come in more often. The final letter in the batch informed him she was pregnant and he was the daddy. *That was me*, she whispered, out loud.

She almost missed a small photo album tucked inside a flannel shirt. Ella was afraid to open it, but when she did, she found pictures from her childhood. Pictures of her father holding her as a baby, with a big, sheepish grin on his face. She didn't recognize the little girl, but it had to be her. Another photo showed her lying on his chest as he slept on the sofa. She wiped her nose on her sleeve, and brushed tears from her cheeks as she quietly wept. The last picture showed her parents in front of a Christmas tree, with her between them, giggling like it was the funniest day ever.

Her father's memories, not hers. How could he do that? How could he leave her? She was just a little girl. There was a gaping hole where her memories should be. She marked the box with a big X to be thrown away. Walter was also inspecting each item in the room. What he couldn't categorize, he peed on.

The room held a treadmill, low miles, like every other house in the world. No curtains on the window. There was a pile of books on a small table, mostly recovery information. Tips on staying sober. That one obviously didn't work. She tossed them into the garbage bag, along with stacks of woodworking magazines.

By now the sun was fully up and Ella grew more anxious waiting for the phone call from the Coroner or Chief Jones to say the autopsy was complete. She took a shower and put on a fresh pair of jeans, a white cotton shirt, canvas hi-tops, and her Cubs hat. With her Glock in the ankle holster, she was ready to go. Her suitcase was packed because she never unpacked, ready to toss in the trunk.

When the phone rang, it startled her, even though she had been expecting it. It was Chief Jones, and he told her to come to police headquarters right away.

She patted Walter on his head as he sat beside her. "Bad news, little buddy. Our time together has come to an end." He had moved on to licking his left paw. "The good news is you're going to spend more time with Jackson Lee in the opulent funeral home where you'll be fed very well and treated like the king you are." She felt tears well up in her eyes. "Damn it. This is why I never wanted a dog."

She stood up and grabbed her suitcase, briefcase, phone, and leash. "Time to hit the road, Walter. I'll be back in Chicago tonight and you'll be sleeping in a different bathroom."

Chapter 10
Autopsy Results
Wednesday Morning

It only took a few minutes for Ella to drop Walter off at the funeral home with Martha. Wednesday morning in Prosper was fairly quiet. As she drove to the police station, a black pickup truck shuddered and rocked around the square belching black smoke from its muffler, and she passed three cars slowly heading out of town. Other than that, the streets were empty.

The big office was full. She joined Chief Jones, Bobby Dean, and Officer Connie, and then was introduced to Junior Wheeler and Big Dick, the Mayor. She was told Junior worked as an intern in the department. The Mayor shook her hand, and smiled. He took up a lot of room. A young patrolman of medium height and build, was already seated. His name was Jim Bob, and he had been working nights. Everyone, except the Medical Examiner from the Georgia Bureau of Investigation, sat down. It was ten-fifteen a.m.

The Medical Examiner stood at the front of the room facing the chairs. Loretta Mae Montgomery wore a long, silk dress embroidered with butterflies, and very tall shoes. Her dark, curly hair was pulled back in a bun.

"Thanks, ya'll, for being prompt," the M.E. began. She leafed through the pages held in her hand, then looked up. "I am Loretta Mae Montgomery, Medical Examiner from the Georgia Bureau of Investigation, Savannah, and my job today is to advise the Prosper Police

Department on the cause and manner of death of the deceased, Ray Flynn, who I autopsied last night."

She eyed the group over her very large, green-rimmed glasses. "For any newbies out there, cause is why. In other words, what is the medical reason, injury, or disease responsible for the death. And manner is how, or the circumstances that led to the death." The crowd was quiet. Ella had heard quite a few autopsy reports, so her attention waned as she checked her iPhone.

Loretta Mae was in her realm. "Mr. Flynn, a fifty-five-year-old male, was found Monday morning at approximately nine-fifteen a.m. after a wellness check by the Prosper Police Department, in response to a concerned citizen call at eight-thirty-six a.m. Apparently, a dog was howling in the house." She removed an enlarged photograph from her papers, and handed it to Chief Jones to pass around the group.

"As you can see from the photograph, Mr. Flynn was found lying on his right side on the sofa. There is no pillow and it does not look like a natural sleeping position." She looked directly at Chief Jones. "Unfortunately, there were very few pictures taken at the scene."

Ella was anxious to see the picture. She agreed with the M.E. There was definitely something odd about the position. Possibly, she thought, he was having chest pain and lay down on the sofa to see if it would stop.

"There was no forced entry and the front door was locked." The M.E. laid her papers on a desk, and picked up a new group. "I have fixed the physiological time of death between two a.m. and two-thirty a.m. The estimated, legal time of death is two-fifteen a.m., Monday morning. And here are the autopsy findings."

Ella checked her watch. Only ten-thirty-five. She'd be in Atlanta by three o'clock this afternoon. Turn in the car, and catch the five o'clock flight to O'Hare. It would be good to be home and back to work.

"To begin. The eyes appeared bloodshot, indicating petechial hemorrhaging. In addition, there was bruising around the nose and mouth."

What? Ella sat up and quickly laid her phone down on the chair next to her. This was not ordinary. She felt her heart quicken.

"I recovered trace evidence, blue fibers, from a corner of the mouth. While there was no external evidence of injury, there were patterned abrasions and contusions of the skin of the anterior neck, and soft tissue injuries on the lower back and legs of the body, indicating Mr. Flynn had been dragged from Point A to the sofa."

Ella was transfixed. The M.E. was saying this wasn't a natural death. She could hear her heart beating in her ears as she came to full attention.

"Cyanosis was evident in the skin and tissues, indicating a progression of asphyxia and oxygen depletion. There was discoloration of the skin. It was dark blue to black. And visceral congestion via dilation of venous blood vessels and blood stasis. There was no fracture of the hyoid bone."

The M.E. paused to gauge the small group's reaction to the findings. Absolute silence. "The cause of death is asphyxia by smothering, or suffocation. Ladies and gentlemen, this is a homicide."

Chapter 11
Homicide
Wednesday morning

After the pronouncement of homicide as the manner of death, the group erupted in loud talk, squeaking chairs against the wall, and began meeting in small groups. Ella was so surprised, she couldn't stand up. She couldn't join in. Her father was murdered. His death was intentional. Who would do that?

Loretta Mae Montgomery offered her hand. "I'm so sorry, Detective Flynn."

She looked up and smiled. "Didn't see that one coming. It's going to take some time to get my head around it."

"I completely understand," she said. "If you have any questions, please give me a call. I'm headed back to Savannah."

Ella watched her leave, then Connie sat down next to her. "I can't believe it. I feel so bad for you."

She smiled at her. "Thanks, Connie. I admit, it's going take some time to absorb this." She surveyed the room. The Mayor was holding court with Chief Jones. She decided that was a good conversation to start with. She excused herself and walked over.

"Chief Jones, Mayor Wheeler," she said, nodding to each man. "This comes as quite a surprise to me. How about you guys?"

"I sure as hell wasn't expecting this, Flynn," the Mayor said. "This is a quiet little town. This kind of thing doesn't happen much here." Remembering her connection to the victim, he added: "Sorry."

"Thanks," she said, and turned to Chief Jones. "What's the plan? Where do we start?"

"Plan? Yes, let's talk about that." The Chief was a take-charge guy with a new mission. He signaled Bobby Dean to come over and join them. "We don't have the manpower to assign someone to the case," he admitted. "Bobby Dean, I need you to talk with the neighbors on that street. Find out what they saw and heard Sunday night going into Monday morning."

Bobby Dean nodded in agreement. "I'll get right on it," he said.

Ella caught the Chief's eye. "Chief, if you don't mind a Chicago cop joining in, I'd like to help out." She leaned her hip against a desk.

"I thought you were anxious to get back to Chicago?"

"Now that this is a murder investigation, I'd like to see what I can contribute." She needed to stay and help. It was important to her.

Chief Jones nodded his head in agreement. "I understand."

"Thanks, Chief," she said. "I have one more day on my two-day bereavement pass, so instead of flying back today, I can leave tomorrow." She looked at the Mayor and Bobby Dean for their reactions. "It might be just enough time to turn something up."

Chief Jones looked at the Mayor. Big Dick had his arms crossed in front of his large abdomen, with a frown on his face. "Don't forget, Chief, you've got Junior here. We don't need Flynn. Junior can take care of it."

The Chief smiled. "I don't think we can compare a young intern to a seasoned Chicago detective. I'd appreciate Flynn's help, even if it is for only one more day. The first forty-eight hours of a homicide investigation are the most important, and we've already lost twenty-hour hours."

Ella smiled back at him. "Thanks, Chief."

The Chief turned to Sgt. Bobby Dean, fidgeting with his phone.

"Cooperate with Detective Flynn, Bobby Dean. Tell her everything you know. Got it?"

"Yes, sir," he said, sliding his phone in his pocket. Ella smiled at him, but his look back was deadpan. She wanted to know more about him.

Ella was planning her next move. "I understand Ray was at a bar Sunday night before he came home. Do you know the name of it?" She looked from the mayor, to Sgt. Bobby Dean, to the Chief. "It was Jake's Bar," they said in unison.

"That's where I'll start," she said. "I'll be in touch." *It's only one more day, but it could just work out.*

The Chief smiled back at her. "Let me know what you find out from Jake."

"I'll do that." Ella was on her way to retrieve Walter for one more day. She already missed him. She opened the door and drove back to the funeral home.

Chapter 12
Picking up Walter again
Wednesday

Walter waddled and wagged, but his face didn't seem to get the message. He looked disappointed, but in a good way. He was either happy to see Ella again, or frankly, disgusted by the entire situation.

Wednesday morning, Jackson Lee was as well-dressed as a funeral director in an expensive dark grey three-piece suit could be. He was not clean-shaven. Ella loved his three-day beard.

"I've come to reclaim my dog. You're working today, I see," she said, "Someday," she said, "I'm going to dress up, too, and you'll be surprised."

Behind his glasses, his hazel eyes squinted when he laughed. "You're beautiful, all the time."

She felt herself blush at the compliment, even though the classiest part of her outfit today was the Cubs hat. "Gee, thanks," she said. "I just came from the autopsy results at the police department."

He waited for her to go on. Walter was tired of standing, so he dropped himself on the floor to rest from standing up.

"It's not a heart attack. It's been ruled a homicide." She couldn't believe she said the words. She didn't want to believe it.

"Oh, no," he said, surprised. "Tell me about it from the top." They sat together in the foyer on an antique fainting sofa.

Her voice wavered when she told him what happened. "The Medical Examiner from the GBI came in this morning, and she gave a report to a group of us at the police station." Ella took a tissue from a box on the table, just in case. "She went through the typical stuff, but it ended with the cause of death, suffocation, and the manner of death, which was homicide."

"That's terrible news. I don't understand," he said, frowning. "Who on earth would kill your father? I don't think he had any enemies." Jackson Lee took another tissue from the box for her, just in case.

Ella surprised herself at her reaction to the news. Tears welled up in her eyes, and she blew her nose. It was more of a honk than blow. *I'll wipe it, instead, next time to cut down on the noise.* She could tell Jackson Lee was trying not to laugh. "Sorry," she said. "I didn't expect to cry."

He held the tissue up. "Go ahead. I'll wait."

She put her head in her hands, and wept. He patted her lightly on her back. It didn't take long. "Honestly, I never cry. This isn't like me at all," she said, when she stopped and wiped her nose. "It's weird, right?"

He smiled, a little half smile. "You're human. It's okay. Everybody cries." Then he added, "Their noses don't usually honk, though."

That made her laugh. "You should hear me sneeze."

"I'm looking forward to it," he brushed the last tear from her cheek. "What happens now?"

"Chief Warner originally gave me a two-day leave, so it's okay if I fly back tomorrow, instead of today. I have one more day to see what I can find out."

"You're not leaving today?" He seemed pleased.

She smiled to herself. *Yup,* she thought, *he definitely likes me.* "No, not today. I'll take custody of Walter, again, if you don't mind."

The dog glanced up when he heard his name, and thumped his tail on the floor. "Seems to be okay with Walter," he said, "so it's fine with me, too."

"I'm going to start with Jake's Bar. That's where my father was

Sunday night. After he left the bar and came home, he was killed." *Still hard to believe.* "Chief Jones has Bobby Dean following up with the neighbors."

Jackson Lee glanced her way. "I've got an idea. Since you're not leaving today, why don't you come for supper? I'd like to make a nice supper for you tonight before you go back to Chicago."

She was surprised. "Connie told me what a great cook you are."

"That was certainly kind of her. Will you come?" He looked her way, expectantly.

"Absolutely. That sounds amazing. What time?" Good, hot food. She was overwhelmed.

"About seven, if that suits you." His smile showed he was definitely pleased.

"Wonderful. Thank you so much. What should I bring?"

He pointed to Walter. "The dog, if you want to. But, if I remember right, he goes to bed early."

"He did last night, curled up on the rug in the bathroom. I'll leave him to guard the house," she joked. "Actually, he closes the bathroom door behind him, so he'll be locked in."

"He does that here, too. I was fixin' to put in a stool and teach him to open the door."

Ella laughed. "Let me know when you do that. I want to watch. I will be here at seven, without our little friend. Right now, I'm off to Jake's Bar." Walter sauntered off toward the door, pulling Ella away from Jackson Lee.

"Looking forward to it," he said, waving goodbye.

She smiled to herself, wondering what a home-cooked meal in the South would be like. Seven o'clock couldn't come soon enough.

Chapter 13
Jake's Bar
Wednesday early afternoon

"Sorry I'm late," Jake said, although he didn't look sorry, just very tired. "Let me open up here."

Jake's Bar was built in the shape of a narrow rectangle and held a few tables and eight stools. It was seedy, at best, and looked like it hadn't been cleaned since the beginning of time. The good part was the back of the bar was well-stocked with liquors and there was beer on tap. *Fully functional*, Ella thought. *What more do you need?*

The inside of the little bar was dingy and dark even in bright daylight and she had to wait for her eyes to become accustomed to it. She handed Jake her Police Department card. "My name is Detective Ella Flynn, with the Chicago Police Department, and I'm here to follow up on the recent death of my father, Ray Flynn." She showed him her Chicago Star. "My cell phone number is on the back of the card in case you need to contact me."

He looked at the card, and turned it over. "Can I get you a draft, detective?"

Her mouth watered just thinking about it. "Although that sounds wonderful, not today. Thanks."

He removed two chairs from the top of a table, and set them in place for the discussion. She grabbed the one closest to her that faced the wooden bar. Walter lay down next to her and promptly nodded off.

"Okay," he said. "Let's get this over with."

She took out a notebook and pen, crossed her legs, and used her ankle as a support. "As I told you when I called a little bit ago, my father's death was ruled a homicide by the Georgia Bureau of Investigation this morning."

His eyes widened. "Yeah, that's ridiculous. I mean, I heard it was a heart attack. What the hell happened?"

Excellent question, she thought. "The police are just now starting the investigation, so we don't know why, or who the killer is. It appears he was suffocated when he got home from your bar early Monday morning."

"Who would do that? Ray never made any trouble." He took a pack of cigarettes out of his breast pocket, and lit one up. The smoke blew directly into Ella's face. She coughed behind her hand.

"That's exactly what I'm trying to find out. And that's why I need your help today." He stubbed out his cigarette on the floor.

"Fire away. Ask me anything."

"Great. I understand my father, Ray Flynn, was here Sunday night. Do you remember about what time he came in, and how long he stayed?"

He chewed on his lower lip as he tapped into his memory. "It wasn't busy yet, so it must have been around five o'clock. By seven, it was packed. It gets so loud in here, you wouldn't believe it."

She nodded her head in agreement, and waited for him to go on.

"When it started to clear out around midnight, I noticed Ray swaying down the hallway to the bathroom. He was loaded, all right."

"Did you notice him talk to anyone while he was here?"

"The only one I remember is a little guy. He comes in here most every night, sat next to him. Ray was hunched over, real close, bending the guy's ear. Then the little guy left all of a sudden."

"Do you know his name?" Ella was writing it all down.

"Yeah, it's Larry something. We just call him Larry-with-the-limp because he's got a gimpy leg." Jake rubbed the stubble on his chin.

"Would you have any idea where he lives?"

Jake shrugged his shoulders. "A lot of guys come in here. I don't get to know them."

"Please," she urged. "Anything you can think of will help."

He thought about it. "Okay, I remember one time he said he lived down by the river. Probably in one of those shanties above the shoreline."

She looked up from her notebook and smiled. "Any little tidbit you can give me is a big help. I'm grateful. Did he talk to anybody else?"

"Sorry, no clue. It gets so busy in here…" Jake seemed done.

Ella recapped their conversation. "So, Ray Flynn came in around five o'clock, got pretty drunk, talked to a guy named Larry-with-the-limp who left, then went home when the bar closed. Is that right?"

"I think I left out the part where Ray passed out on the bar. I had to wake him up at two o'clock to close up."

"Was that something he normally did?"

"Hell no. He'd have a couple of drinks and go on home."

"Why do you think he was drinking so much?"

"Well, he acted like he was real scared when he came in. Had a few shots."

"Did he usually drink shots?"

"No, ma'am. Jack and coke."

"Do you think he was drinking because he was afraid of something?"

"I know he saw something that scared him. He told me."

Ella wrote that down. "Was there anybody else in the bar at that time?"

"Nah, it was empty, except for me and Ray."

"Did you notice anyone outside?"

"Nope."

"All right, it was just you and Ray," Ella agreed. "Then he walked home and somebody killed him. Do you have any idea who would do that?"

Jake sat back in his chair. "No. I don't know why anybody would kill him. It don't make sense to me." He seemed lost in thought. "Did I tell you he kept saying 'you won't believe what I saw'?"

Ella looked up and stopped writing. "What else did he say?"

"He acted like he wanted to tell me something, but changed his mind. He said I wouldn't believe it anyway."

"He saw something, and he was afraid to tell you about it?" She needed to be absolutely clear on this.

Jake glanced at the floor, then kicked the cigarette butt under the table. "Let me think about it." He paused. "Okay, that's what he said. 'You won't believe what I saw.'"

"He seemed scared?"

"Terrified. I don't think I've seen him get that drunk before."

"I wonder what he saw that caused this reaction?" she pondered, chewing on the end of her pen. "Can you think of anything?"

"No clue, but it had to be really, really bad to scare Ray like that."

"I agree. Maybe Larry-with-the-limp can tell us."

"I hope you find him. Why the hell would anybody kill Ray Flynn?"

She closed her notebook. "You hit the nail on the head. Where's the motive?" Since it was likely that was all she was going to get, she picked up her phone, notebook, and Walter's leash, and stood up. "Thanks. You've been a tremendous help. If you think of anything else, anything at all, call me." She extended her hand.

He stood up, too, and grabbed her hand. "Come back for that

beer."

"I believe I will," she answered, waving as Walter led her outside. The transition from dark to light made her eyes squint and water. The sky was clear, the air was humid, and the sun was hot. Another summer day in Georgia.

She looked at a text from Chief Jones on her phone. The next stop was back to the police station.

Chapter 14
Bobby Dean Solves the Crime
Wednesday afternoon

Bobby Dean couldn't have looked more pleased with himself than he did right now. He was regaling the Chief with a long, somewhat involved story that included hand gestures and high- fives.

When they noticed Ella and Walter come in, they waved her over. The group included Junior Wheeler and Officer Connie.

"Great news, Flynn," the Chief said. "Bobby Dean collared the little slime ball that killed your father."

Ella was stunned into silence for the second time that day. "What?"

"Really. Seriously. Go on Bobby Dean, tell her."

She had only been gone a few hours. She sat down at a desk while Walter walked in a circle until he collapsed in a heap. Snoring. "Yeah, tell me all about it," she said. This was definitely going to be interesting.

Bobby Dean made himself comfortable leaning against a desk, ankles crossed, a smug smile on his sallow face. "I was fixin' to bang on some doors when I remembered what I forgot." He paused for effect. "I was working Sunday night, the night of the burglary, when Ray got himself killed."

Ella sat very still. "I see. And what did you remember?"

"When I was driving through the neighborhood, I saw a guy wearing a hoodie, walking head down. Turned into a front yard quick and I couldn't see him anymore. Well, I got a call right then, so I forgot I seen him."

The Chief was smiling a big, wide smile. "Go on, tell her," he encouraged him.

Bobby Dean was barely able to contain his excitement. "We ran the prints we found on broken glass at the Gabriel house and came up with Anthony Vainisi. Wanted on a warrant out of Jessup for prior residential burglary." He snapped his pen in and out, in and out, in a staccato rhythm. "And I said, that's our guy. I bet my life on it."

Ella leaned back in her chair and crossed one leg over the other. "That's some great police work, Bobby Dean." She smiled.

Chief Jones couldn't hold back anymore. "Not just the burglary, it's the guy who killed your father, too."

Bobby Dean was on a roll. "That front yard I told you about? That he turned into. It was Ray's house."

"Hmm." Ella said, pursing her lips. "That's a pretty big leap from residential burglary to murder. Why do you think he did that?" It sounded unlikely to her, but she didn't want to ruin Bobby Dean's big moment.

"We figure it was his second burglary that night and it went wrong." The Chief nodded his head in agreement with what Bobby Dean was saying. "He probably saw Ray come home and slipped into the house behind him."

The Chief slapped his hand on the desk. "We've got him at the scene of the crime. At two o'clock in the morning. Slam bang," he said. They were all obviously pleased with the outcome.

Ella nodded her head in agreement. "All right, then, have you picked him up yet?" She looked from the Chief to Bobby Dean.

"We're on our way to Jessup right now," the Chief said. "They're holding him for us, but we wanted to let you know right away so you can clear your mind about who killed your father, and get on back to Chicago."

"Thanks, Chief. You think this is the right guy?" She trusted him.

"I do, Flynn," he confirmed. "If Bobby Dean saw him there, at your father's house, at two in the morning, then I'll go along with it." He turned to Sgt. Bobby Dean. "You wouldn't lie to me, would you Bobby Dean?"

He was taken by surprise. "No, Chief." His eyes were wide. Ella was curious about his reaction. He was either taken by surprise, or lying his ass off. She'd remember this.

The Chief smiled. "I was just checking. That's all."

"I'll be sorry to see you go," Connie said to her.

Ella smiled. "I'll still be here tomorrow for a while." She planned to look for the elusive Larry-with-the-limp down by the river before she left for Chicago. She hadn't mentioned his existence to Chief Jones, mostly because there hadn't been an opportunity to tell him what she learned from talking with Jake. She intended to keep it to herself for now and see where it led, since they were confident they arrested the right guy.

She reached down and grabbed Walter's leash on the floor, and shook him awake. "Come on, Buddy, time to go." He shook his head until his long ears flapped around and smacked him in the face. He was ready to go.

"You'll let me know if anything changes?"

Chief Jones nodded and smiled.

"I'll stop by tomorrow sometime, before I go home."

Walter was headed toward the door already, pulling Ella behind him like a sled. Her intuition told her there was more to the arrest than she knew. She would keep her mind open to any possibilities.

Chapter 16
More about Bobby Dean
Wednesday afternoon

Ella pulled up to the little brown house at the dead-end of School Street. Connie had been right. It was in bad shape. The front porch was hanging at an angle, and a post was separated from what it was holding up.

Dixie turned out to be the opposite of Connie. Short where Connie was tall, and wide where Connie was lean. Dressed in yellow overalls and armed with a big hammer, she invited Ella in.

"Connie told me you were on your way," she said. "Can I get you something to drink?"

"No ma'am," Ella said. Because it was late in the day, she expected it to be a fairly quick interview. She tiptoed carefully on the few sturdy floorboards available that led to an aluminum chair that was pointed out. She could see straight down to the concrete foundation.

"Thank you so much for seeing me on short notice like this. I'm sure Connie told you I'm Detective Ella Flynn with the Chicago Police Department, down here because my father died." She had to think about it. "He didn't die as much as someone killed him, which is what I found out this morning."

Dixie nodded, her head full of bright bottle-red curls. "Connie told me. Awful. That's just awful. I feel terrible for you. And please call me Dixie," she said, with a bright smile.

She handed Dixie her card with the cell phone number written on the back. "Just in case you think of something you want to tell me after I leave."

"Thanks," She shoved it in her pocket.

"Okay, Dixie." Ella opened her notebook and got her pen ready. She glanced in her direction, saw her perched on a similar aluminum chair in the corner. "I just found out Chief Jones and Bobby Dean have arrested a residential burglar who was in the area Monday morning around two a.m., and charged him with my father's homicide, in addition to the burglary down the street. I guess the crime has been solved, I'm happy to say." She wanted to back the police up on the arrest, but keep her eyes open for pieces of the puzzle that didn't fit.

Dixie's eyes widened. "That's amazing. That was quick."

"Yes, it was," Ella agreed. "I'm going back to Chicago tomorrow, but I wanted to tie up a few loose ends just for myself." *As long as I have the time and opportunity, it won't hurt to learn more about Bobby Dean. Even if I never put it to good use.*

"I was wondering what you could tell me about Bobby Dean. Connie told me, at one time, you were both in foster care at the Catholic Church." She looked at Dixie expectantly, her pen hovering over the paper.

Dixie rolled her eyes and shook her head. "What can I tell you about that clusterfuck... I had been in at least ten foster homes by the time I was fourteen. That was when Father Santos brought me on board at the Catholic Church."

"He sounds like a great guy." It was a leading question.

"That is definitely what he'd like you to think. Charming like crazy to other people, but not like that to the foster kids." Dixie frowned as she remembered it.

"How many foster kids were there with you?"

"Besides me, there was Bobby Dean, and another girl. I've forgotten her name. Bobby Dean had already been there for a couple of years." She chewed her lower lip. "He might have been eight or nine when he moved in."

"Does the Priest still take care of foster kids?" If he did, Ella planned to check on them.

"Not as far as I know. I think we were the last ones." She fidgeted in her chair. "Bobby Dean stayed there because he was terrified to leave. I was terrified to stay." Ella didn't want her to talk about it, if she didn't want to.

"I really appreciate your honesty, Dixie. I'll try to be brief. What was the relationship like between Father Santos and Bobby Dean?"

She bit her lip. "He treated him like a dog. Made Bobby Dean do things nobody else wanted to do. Bury the cat, kill a chicken. The bastard would scream at him and tell him what a worthless piece of shit he was. The kid would walk with his head down all the time. Never look me in the eye. He turned Bobby Dean into that person, scared all the time," she said, angrily.

"That's awful. Why did Bobby Dean go along with it? Why didn't he leave?" Ella realized he had no other place to go, but she wanted to know what Dixie thought about it.

"No choice. Father Santos would scream at him about how stupid he was and how nobody wanted him, except for him. How he gave him a life and an education, and now he had to pay him back." Her eyes were dark. "You owe me!" he said, over and over."

Gaslighting, emotional and verbal abuse. Father Santos sounded like a sociopath. "Did he physically abuse him, too?"

"Like a punching bag. Always hitting him where it wouldn't be obvious to the people in the church. He didn't want them to know," Dixie said. "To the congregation, he was a great guy, or so they thought. I stayed as far away from him as I could."

"How long did you stay there?" It sounded like a terrible place.

"About six months." Dixie half-smiled. "If nothing else, I'm street smart. I've spent years running from foster parents who raped me, beat me. When he started sucking up to me, I knew what he had in mind. My days were numbered, so I left." She shuddered as if there was a sudden cold draft.

Ella knew she'd barely scratched the surface of the abuse Dixie had suffered, so she changed the subject. "And Bobby Dean stayed. He could have called the police, right?"

Dixie smirked. "Who would they believe? A priest or a foster kid? His congregation thought the sun rose and set on Father Santos."

"I see that." The police usually believed the adult.

"I think he was convinced he was too stupid to live on his own," Dixie explained. "When he got a job with the police department, he felt a little better about himself. The Chief is helping him. But he still lives with Father Santos."

She felt really bad for them both. "I'm sure this isn't the life he would have chosen." She closed her notebook. "I think I'm finished here. I'll let you get back to your rehabbing." It was easier to understand Bobby Dean knowing his background. She wished she could do something about Father Santos. *If I was eight again, I'd kick him in the nuts*, she thought, and smiled to herself.

"By the way, what happened to other girl?" Ella asked, on the way out.

"Beats me," Dixie said. "One day she just wasn't there anymore."

Ella stopped walking. "What do you think happened to her?"

"She could have run away like I did. Or, something bad could have happened to her." Dixie kicked a stone out of her way. "I guess we'll never know."

"I suppose not," Ella agreed. There wouldn't be any time to look into it, anyway. "So long, Dixie," she said, waving goodbye. "Thanks for your help."

In the car, when she reviewed her notes, it was easy to see how the constant abuse from Father Santos impacted the anxious young man. Since he still lived with the Priest, she wondered what hold the Priest had over Bobby Dean, if any. She wished she could stay, for more than this reason. Jackson Lee was on her mind.

Chapter 17
Supper and Smooth Jazz
Wednesday night

When Ella dressed for supper, she mentally patted herself on the back for bringing a summer dress. She always packed too many clothes, but in this case, it paid off.

The yellow cotton dress had a low-cut neckline, and it wasn't too short, but definitely short enough to show off the ankle holster, so she put her Glock in her purse. She wore her dark hair long and curly, tucked behind her ears. She left her Cubs hat on the table.

Whether to bring Walter. He had eaten his supper and surveyed his kingdom, and was now content to lie on the rug in the bathroom. He was out for the night.

The thought of a home-cooked meal made her mouth water. She was eager to know Jackson Lee better since they seemed to have a lot in common. She wanted to bounce her investigation theories off him.

She walked the few blocks to the funeral home. The afternoon light was changing to golden and russet hues, the shadows deepening. Quiet streets. Inside the houses, lights were on for supper and she could see the people in their kitchens and on their porches. She heard the wail of a faraway train.

Ella walked up to the back door and knocked, pleased to see Jackson Lee open the door wearing a t-shirt, frilly apron, and shorts. "Nice knees," she said.

"Thanks. They're my father's," he said, with a big smile. "You look like a sunflower, Ella." He took her hand casually and gave her a quick hug. "Please come in and make yourself at home."

"You are too kind, sir." The vintage kitchen had a big sink, modern stove, and two huge built-in china cabinets. The aroma that wafted from the stove was tantalizing, serving to make her even hungrier.

She pulled out one of the four chairs placed around a round wooden table, and tossed her purse on it. "Thanks for inviting me. I was hungry enough to eat Walter's food."

"Delighted you could come." He turned back to the stove. "I hope you like shrimp and grits."

She nodded her head. "I'd like grits more if I knew what it was. Sounds gravelly."

He feigned astonishment. "You've never eaten grits?"

"Nope. Chicago hot dogs, Chicago deep dish pizza, and Chicago steaks. No grits."

"Grits are just crushed, dried cornmeal cooked with my secret ingredients, including a cheesy sauce and tasty spices," he explained, pointing to the pans on the stove. "But, that's not all." He smiled. "Expertly cooked zesty, smoky shrimp and bacon with Cajun hot sauce to top them off." It smelled wonderful. "I'm fixin' to make the collard greens now, and cornbread is in the oven." He seemed very proud of himself.

Ella was impressed. "You are quite a cook. Everything smells amazing."

"I know," he agreed. "Real Southern comfort food. Now, what would you like to drink? Wine, beer, bourbon?" They agreed on a bottle of Chardonnay, not being educated on what went with Shrimp and Grits. He popped the cork like he had done it a few times before, and poured two glasses. He handed one to Ella.

She took a sip. "This is delicious, smooth and rich. Does it come in gallon containers, or can I drink it out of the bottle?" She hoped he knew she was kidding.

Jackson Lee took a sip, too. "It's from the Flowers Winery on the west coast. I can probably get you a gallon bottle with a spigot on the side, but if you drink it out of the bottle, I won't have to wash a glass. Would that work?"

Ella smiled. She loved his sense of humor. "If that's all you've got, then I guess it's okay." She sat back and sipped her wine.

Ella watched Jackson Lee turn on an ancient turntable and center a disc on it. His black-rimmed glasses, his beard, just long enough to be soft, and his smile fit so well together. Subtly, the sexy strains of Kenny G's *Songbird* filtered through the room as he adjusted the volume. "Do you like smooth jazz?" he asked.

"Very much." She smiled.

He held his arms out to welcome her. "Dance?"

She nodded, slid her sandals off, then strolled seductively over to him. She lightly curved her hand on the back of his neck. He placed his left hand on the small of her back, and with his other hand, gently drew her close until they could feel each other's heartbeat through their light, summer clothing.

They swayed to the music, holding each other tight, enjoying the warmth and sensual touch of each other's body. It set off every reaction in her body, from aching desire to lust. They fit so well together. She rested her head on his shoulder, captured by the rhythm and the moment. His soft stubble brushed her cheek. *He smells so good.* The record finished, but they didn't move. He absently ran his fingers through the length of her hair, and avoided her look.

"I'd better get back to cookin'," he said, but still held her in his arms.

Ella was very warm. She rubbed her cheeks with the palms of her hands, and broke away. They both went to retrieve their wine glasses. She glanced at him as she sipped. He seemed flustered, too.

He raised his glass. "Let's toast to this occasion." His eyes behind his glasses were a lighter hue of blue-green. *His smile is so sexy*, she thought. Chris Botti was playing sax in the background.

"What if we toast to supper and smooth jazz?" she said.

He clinked his glass on hers in agreement. "Great idea. Thank you for coming, and for the pleasure of your company. I'm very glad you didn't leave today." His eyes studied her, and hers dared him to come closer. A timer beeped in the background, breaking their concentration. He returned to the stove, and sighed.

Ella sat back down again, flushed and excited by the way he made her feel. "Thanks for inviting me," she said. "It was nice of you to think of me, alone in town with only canned food to eat."

He turned and smiled. "My pleasure." He sipped his wine, and continued preparing supper.

"Do you have any Barry White?" she asked.

He rubbed his knuckles against his beard. "I don't believe I do."

"Thank heaven," she said, smiling. "That would have pushed me over the edge."

He started arranging the plates on the table to serve supper. He smiled, seductively. "I guarantee I will have Barry White next time." *He thinks there will be a next time*, she thought. *I hope so.*

"What did you do today?" he asked her.

"I was pretty busy. Walter and I went through my father's stuff this morning. He had lots of fishing equipment. Would you like it? Otherwise, I'll give it away."

He delivered the final plate, then sat across from her. "A man cannot have enough fishing equipment. Sure, I'll take it. Now, tell me what you think of the grits." He waited anxiously for her to take a bite.

"Amazing. Delicious and just a little spicy. My new favorite food." Her eyes watered a little from the hot sauce, but her tongue loved it. "You are an awesome cook."

He seemed pleased, and smiled. They ate in silence, the music in the background their accompaniment. When they finished, and the dishes were washed, they moved to the sofa with a new bottle of wine. "I've got a surprise for you," he said, turning on the TV. "For your viewing pleasure tonight, 'Major League.'"

She laughed. "You remembered."

He sat close to her and put his arm around her shoulders. "I love movies. What about you?"

"Yes," she admitted. "A good movie, popcorn, lying on the sofa. I love that." When he sat back, she rested her head on his chest. He was making it very hard to think of going back to Chicago.

Sometime during the movie, he held her hand and they moved even closer together. Ella looked up at him and he bent to kiss her. She was surprised by the warmth of his mouth when his lips parted, she eagerly kissed him back. She wasn't sure if it was the wine, or the way his voice changed to deep and husky that made her so thirsty for the taste of him. She didn't want to stop.

"Wow," she said, breathless, avoiding his eyes.

"Yes, my thoughts exactly," he said, smiling. His glasses had fogged up, and he rubbed the lenses with the bottom of his shirt.

"I'm going to leave tomorrow." She couldn't help but smile back.

"What if you didn't?" he asked. "What if you stayed here?"

She thought about it. "I wouldn't have a job, for one thing. But, I suppose I could get used to the crappy, blue house, and I love Walter."

"I want you to stay," he said.

She smiled. "My career is in Chicago, although being with you makes me want to stay here. I can't." She laughed. "I only met you yesterday. You don't even know me."

"I know everything I need to," he said, kissing her softly on the lips. "I know you like dogs, even though you don't want to. I know you enjoy my cooking."

"That's true."

"You're so pretty," he continued. "But you don't wear it like a crown." Ella blushed and looked down. She wasn't used to being complimented on her appearance. It would be very bad to do that at the police department. She thought of herself as one of the guys.

"Thank you for saying that, but you don't really know me. I have a really hard time trusting people."

"Yes," he agreed. "That's the part that takes time, isn't it?"

"More than a day or two."

That was when he leaned in and kissed her even more passionately. She was not able to resist. She thought her heart might stop, but she didn't pull away. He drew her close to him. *This is indescribable,* she thought.

He took her hand. "Let's go sit on the swing. There's a nice breeze tonight. They sat close together, rocking the swing comfortably slow.

"I ate at the Sunshine Café last night. With Connie," she told him.

"My bingo partner Connie? That's nice," he said.

"She's a real character, isn't she?"

"Definitely. If you want to know something, just ask Connie," he explained. "Even if you don't want to know something, she'll tell you." He chuckled thinking about it.

"She told you about Bobby Dean arresting my father's killer?" She glanced at him, but he was busy pouring more wine.

"She did."

"I figured she did. I'm still on the fence, not sure if it's the right guy." She sighed. "I talked with Jake at his bar this afternoon, and he told me my father seemed to be frightened and worried about something he saw. He said, 'You'll never believe what I saw,' or something to that effect."

He frowned. "Your father saw something that scared him. Do you think that had something to do with his death?"

"It might." She shrugged her shoulders. "Jake said there was a guy in the bar that my father talked to, so if I can find him, hopefully he'll know what happened." It would be so easy if she knew where he was.

"What's his name?"

"They call him Larry-with-the-limp because he's got a bad leg."

He scratched his chin stubble. "No, I've never heard of him. New to me. The police are saying your father went home from Jake's Bar and a burglar killed him."

"Weird, right?"

"Was there evidence of a struggle?" He handed a glass of wine to her.

She took a sip. "No, and after he was killed, his body was dragged to the sofa and staged. A burglar wouldn't bother. He'd run. Besides, where's the motive? He lived in a rundown house. No reason to break in, much less murder someone." *All excellent points*, she thought.

Jackson Lee looked pensive. "It could have been a crime of opportunity. There is such a thing, isn't there?"

"Yes. There could have been no motive, just opportunity. Thanks for pointing that out." She gave him a thumbs up.

Jackson Lee relaxed on the swing. "What's your next step, detective?"

Ella considered the question. "Jake thinks Larry lives down by the river, possibly in a shanty just above the shoreline. I need to talk to him, definitely. Will you take me fishing tomorrow?"

"Fishing?" They both laughed. "It's a date," he said. "Then we can drive up and down the dirt roads by the river and look for Larry-with-the-Limp. Right?"

"That's the plan, Stan," she said. "And before you open another bottle of wine, I should go home to my dog."

He was quiet. "I don't want you to go." He gently kissed her. His mouth was warm and willing. She relaxed against him, kissed him back, then she stood up.

"I really have to go." She avoided looking at him. "I'll get my purse." She walked into the kitchen. Starting a relationship with him that would end a day later, was a really terrible idea.

Jackson Lee was waiting for her on the porch, and silently took her hand as they started down the sidewalk to the blue house. The leaves fluttered in the passing of a gentle wind that casually stroked Ella's long hair. The night was without a sound, except for their footsteps.

"When I drove into town yesterday, I was not impressed. I was a snob." Ella looked down at her feet. "It's weird that in only a day or two, my perspective has changed."

"I'm glad it has." He squeezed her hand.

"I've come to appreciate this charming little town with its curious people."

He laughed. "Are you talking about me?"

"No." She laughed, too. "I'm talking about the police chief that wants to solve everybody's problems, and Connie, and everybody at the café. It's not just the people, it's the glue that holds everybody together. That's what I like. The symmetry."

"I've never heard Prosper described like that, but I do agree with you. When we go fishing tomorrow down by the bridge, you'll like it even more." He nodded his head, walking down the last sidewalk to the blue house. He seemed very sure about it.

As expected, Walter greeted them with howling that could be heard several towns away.

"What time tomorrow?" he asked, as she unlocked the door.

"How about eight o'clock? Do the fish get up early?"

"Depends. Anytime is good."

"Great," she said. "Bring a really big bobber for me."

"This is river fishing." He laughed out loud.

She reconsidered. "All right, then. Bring two bobbers."

"Sounds great," he said, kissing her goodbye, and releasing her hand. "See you tomorrow morning."

She went inside the house, watching Jackson Lee walk away. She was so confused, all she could do was pat Walter on the head until he stopped howling.

Chapter 18
The Altamaha River

Ray's Story
1985

Ray Flynn dropped his backpack on the ground and scanned the Railroad Trestle Bridge over the Altamaha River. It didn't look any worse for wear; it had been rundown for years. It was a big deal in the Civil War, but that was a very long time ago. He wasn't even sure if trains used the track anymore.

Every year, since they were kids, the three of them would meet at the bridge after the school year ended. It was a one-time only, annual event that ended with this final adventure. They graduated from high school three days ago, and everyone was moving on.

He was the first to arrive, Bud and Larry were on their way. They would travel across the bridge into the coastal plains on the other side. Years ago, the Alachua Indian Path crossed the river here, so their quest involved finding arrowheads, bones, and other interesting artifacts. They had amassed a treasure trove of trinkets, but it was much more fun when they were kids. Ray sighed, and tossed a stick out of his way.

The rustling of brush announced Larry's entry into the glen, followed by Bud, who was at least one-half-foot taller than his diminutive friend. Larry's backpack slid off his shoulder and fell at his feet, while Bud squatted and opened his. He took out a folded straight razor, flipped it open, and admired the way the sun glinted off the steel. It was as sharp as a scalpel. He put it in his back pocket, zipped up the backpack, and stood up. Ray was wary about the razor in Bud's hands. Through the years he had become more brazen, more apt to do dangerous things. He wondered what Bud would do today.

Perched hawk-like on a log, wearing baggy yellow shorts and a t-shirt that barely reached her navel, was Skeeter, who had followed Ray there.

"Aw, shit," Larry said. "What's she doing here?"

Without missing a beat, Skeeter scooped up a rock and threw it at Larry's head. It missed, but not by much. Larry gave her a middle finger salute.

Ray laughed. "She could have hit you if she wanted to. I've seen her knock a bird out of the sky."

Skeeter smiled at his praise. She never talked, she just followed Ray. It seemed to him that she was never there. And then she was always there. "I came out of the house this morning, and there she was," he said, pointing to Skeeter. "Sitting on a stump like now, waiting for me. She followed me here."

Bud chuckled. "I think she loves you. L-O-V-E," he said, spelling the word out slow. He dug through his backpack again and came up with a candy bar, half-melted, but easy enough to eat.

"Aw, she doesn't love me. She's just a kid," he said. She told him she was fourteen, but she looked younger because she was so small. Her shoulders were bony and her unwashed blonde hair hung listlessly past her chin. She also told him she was a flower fairy, and her name really was Antonella Hummingbird. She slept inside the drooping bell of the primrose. Ray took it with a grain of salt. She probably had a shitty home life like he did and was escaping reality for a while. Fairy or not, he liked her.

Skeeter carefully arranged two flattened pieces of grass inside her thumbs. She blew between the blades of grass, puffing out her cheeks, until they all heard a long, mournful whistle. Ray didn't like it. To him, it sounded like a call to the gods of perdition.

"What's with the boots?" Larry asked, pointing to Skeeter's feet.

Ray glanced over at her, and shrugged. "She was barefoot," he explained. "She couldn't come with us without any shoes. Anyway, they're my dad's boots. He was passed out drunk on the sofa. They're just a little roomy, is all." He had tied the boots onto Skeeter's feet with rope he had found behind the house. "They'll do."

Bud took a long look across the old bridge. "Any trains still use this bridge?"

"Maybe, maybe not," Ray answered.

"I never saw one," Larry said, slapping a gnat off his forehead.

"If a freight train is still using this track, there's no rhyme or reason when it'll come. You just better not be on the bridge if it does," Ray added.

"From when you see the light of the train, you've got sixty seconds to get off the tracks." Skeeter said, in an ominous voice barely above a whisper. "That ain't much time."

There was silence. Nobody had heard her speak before.

"We'll keep that in mind," Bud said, sarcastically. "Everybody knows that."

Ray pointed to the cypress trees by the bank of the river, silver gray Spanish moss eerily hanging from the branches, breeze tossing it, making it shiver with sunlight. "You see that bare tree there? The one that doesn't have moss hanging from it?"

They all spotted the tree. "So, what?" Larry asked.

"That means somebody was hung from that tree. Moss don't grow on trees dead people swung on." He spat in the weeds.

"Bull shit," Bud said. Larry agreed.

Ray looked him in the eyes. "You don't know that, Bud. "I think they hung a horse thief there." He pulled a white t-shirt out of his backpack and slipped it over his head. He'd always rather be bare chested, except when bugs were involved. "Well, I'm ready. Anybody going with me?"

Bud was fidgeting with a thick stick he found, slapping it on the ground, whipping it on the bushes, bringing out a swarm of angry gnats. He ran from them onto the bridge. "Let's get this show on the road," he shouted. He said that every summer. "I've got places to be."

"I hear that," Ray said, lifting his backpack to his shoulder. Skeeter took her place behind him, and Larry went last. The four moved onto the railroad tracks and felt the wind become strong and gusty, whistling through the girders. They began the long walk across the river.

Ray turned around and saw Skeeter stomp her big boots on the wooden bridge, watching little clouds of dirt rise and fall. She had fallen behind and he went back to help her catch up.

Bud was in the lead. He was punching at the tracks, and the spaces between, with his new stick. Ray knew that in Bud's mind, he was the leader of the group.

Bud was a liar, that's what troubled Ray about his childhood friend. He lied when it wasn't necessary to lie. His stories were the biggest and the best, his lies, giant webs of nonsense. Bud never changed his story. Never admitted he lied. And never, ever admitted he was wrong. Ray didn't think Bud knew what truth was.

He watched Bud set a quick pace across the bridge, expecting the others to follow. They lagged, sputtered, and flitted along, while he yelled for them to hurry. Skeeter stumbled along with the big boots strapped to her skinny legs. Ray stopped again to help her.

"Take it easy, Bud," he yelled into the wind. "Skeeter's dragging these boots."

Larry whistled low. "If she can't keep up, just let her be. Nobody wanted her to come."

Ray gave him a dirty look. "Shut up, asshole." He finished tying Skeeter's boots again and helped her up. "Go on. We'll catch up."

In the middle of the bridge, Larry shifted his backpack from one shoulder to the other, and took out his pig sticker in case they ran into feral hogs. He banged it on the metal foundation of the bridge. Ray noticed his bad leg was limiting his speed over the bridge, and saw Larry rest his body against a girder. The bad leg kept him out of sports, but he hung around with Ray at football practice anyway. He enjoyed the notoriety of being the Quarterback's friend. He was aware of this and tried to find jobs for Larry to do. He was a good friend. Dependable. Most nights, he ate supper at his house and even slept there occasionally. Larry's short temper was easily overlooked.

Midway across the bridge, and on the right side, Ray pointed out a small metal gangplank sitting parallel to the tracks. "It's the only way off the tracks if a train comes," he told Skeeter, certain that a train wouldn't come. "You have to hang onto a girder." She nodded her head, acknowledging that she heard him. The incessant wind made it hard to hear.

Ray surveyed the tracks ahead and was startled Bud was nowhere in sight. He couldn't have reached the end of the bridge already. "Where are you, Bud?" he yelled, anxious, concerned.

"Help," he heard Bud respond, but he didn't see him. "I fell off the bridge." He spotted him about three-quarters of the way across the bridge on the east side, hanging onto a metal ledge with just the river below, swinging in the wind.

"Hang on, I'm coming," Ray screamed, as he sprinted into the gusting wind. When he reached him, he grabbed Bud's arm and hoisted him back on the bridge in a single move. Bud lay on the bridge laughing hysterically, like a circus clown.

"I was just screwing with you," Bud said, with a big smile. "I knew you'd save me."

Ray was furious. "I should throw you off the bridge for doing that." His face was red and his fists were clenched. It took all of his control to keep from punching him. He quickly turned and walked back to the group, the wind against his back now. He had run out of patience with Bud.

The wind had increased in intensity, and the walk across the bridge seemed to be taking much longer than necessary. Bud turned around and shouted to the group behind him. "Can't you assholes move any faster?" He was impatient, slapping the bridge with his wooden stick. The delay was cutting into valuable hiking time, Ray knew. Patience was not a virtue Bud was keen on.

They ignored him. Skeeter took giant steps in the boots to make Ray laugh. She was such an odd girl. Like a completely different species. Though he wouldn't admit it, he enjoyed her company. He'd never had a girl as a friend before.

Ray lived with his alcoholic father who flicked cigarettes at him to wake him up when he fell asleep on the sofa. He didn't respond, except to move away. In his head, he screamed. But in reality, he was mute. The anger festered inside him. He had been taking care of himself forever and was anxious to put a few hundred miles between his father and him. Let somebody else take care of the old drunk.

He had received a football scholarship from the University of Georgia that included housing and food, and the thought of leaving Prosper, Georgia, was first and foremost on his mind. His goal in life was to never come back to the dirty, little town.

"Watch out for hogs," Bud called out, still thinking he was leading the party. "They'll chew your leg off." He had already reached the end of the bridge and squatted in the dirt, investigating his backpack for other treasures he brought.

Ray watched Larry re-examine his backpack, probably looking for his pig stick. He jammed it into his back pocket, and Ray hoped he wouldn't stab himself in the rear-end. He knew he had a bag for snakes, too.

"Keep up!" Bud demanded, but the wind carelessly tore his words away. The small caravan picked up speed finally, until the stragglers reached the end of the bridge and crossed into the brush. The wind stopped there and the heat immediately rose to a furious temperature. Ray stepped off the bridge and noticed stormy dark, grey clouds gathering in the west. He hoped the storm would wait for later in the day.

By the time the four hikers reached the first bend, they were mired in a marsh from recent rains, with mud that threatened to suck their boots off with each step they took. The brambles buzzed with life. Rising like little bits of pepper, the bugs helicoptered onto Larry's wet neck and drilled for blood. He smacked at them weakly, and plodded on. They all wore scarves and hats as a defense.

Their first stop was beyond the edge of previously explored territory. It appeared rich with buried treasure, and last year they agreed to save it for the final trip. Armed, each with his weapon of choice, Larry and Bud fanned out to locate the premier place to start digging. Ray found his own spot far away from the other two, and Skeeter joined him.

His favorite tool was a simple garden trowel he found in the junkyard years ago. He kept the front edge sharp to dig deep in the dirt. Skeeter chose her own tool and dug her own hole. It was quiet as they all concentrated on sorting the dirt and the rocks out from something interesting. The first victory yell was from Larry, who held up a well-formed granite arrowhead. He quickly dug more holes. Ray methodically removed dirt, checked it carefully, and dug again. The morning wore on, the sun rose higher, and they were all drenched in sweat. They agreed to move on.

When they reached the dry, flat summit of the hill, it was time for lunch. They each located a dining spot on the dry ground, and foraged in their backpack for food and drink. The humidity had risen from uncomfortable to overwhelming, and clouds had become threatening.

Ray handed a sandwich to Skeeter, who ate it whole. He glanced at Bud. "What did you decide about the Seminary?"

"Bud smiled and cocked his head. "I'm trying to make my parents love me. They've spent my entire childhood hating me and wishing I was dead. My mother told me that a few years ago after my father whipped me with his belt. I'm making one final effort. I registered at a Seminary in Buffalo, New York. I'm going to be a Priest."

"So much for the Catholic religion," Larry said, and laughed out loud. "Nasty old Bud, a priest."

Bud's eyes squinted and turned black. He picked up the largest rock he could find and threw it at Larry. It hit him in the chest. Larry wheezed in pain, falling forward.

Ray was on his feet, standing over Bud. He tried to keep his voice steady. "That's it," he said. "That's the final straw." Bud didn't say anything. He just kept smiling. He knelt by Larry, to make sure he was all right.

Skeeter had removed the annoying big boots. Her feet were free and she began to dance uninhibited in the Georgia dirt, kicking dust into the wet air. Free from her boots, free from her mother, free from the house. Antonella Hummingbird was a flower fairy again.

"It's gonna rain," she said, pointing to the sky.

The clouds had become larger and closer. Bud was sweeping the flat hill with his stick, looking for nonexistent landmines, and using his straight razor to cut ants in half. He was on the lookout for larger vermin to slice and dice.

"We should probably head back," Ray said.

"Nah, it's early," Bud said, and resumed his mission.

In the distance, they could see strokes of lightning and hear a faint rumbling. "Time to go," Ray said. "I want to get across the bridge before the storm hits." Skeeter sat down and let him tie her boots back on. He picked up his backpack and together they started back to the railroad trestle bridge. Larry followed.

Bud tossed his stick away and zipped up his backpack. He positioned it on one shoulder and caught up to the hikers. "This was a complete waste of time."

Ray, Skeeter, Larry, and Bud moved swiftly down the path and around the bends. When they stepped foot on the wooden slats of the bridge, thunder covered up the scream of an oncoming freight train.

The sky blackened, blotting out the sun. Rumbles were louder now. Random darts of lightning, and *basso profundo* thunder announced the arrival of rain pellets. The wind violently returned and buffeted the group, rocking them from one side to the other, forcing them to slow down to avoid the empty spaces between each slatted railroad tie.

Too late now, with heads bent, the group hurriedly scrambled across the bridge, unaware of the bright train light behind them, barely visible through the rain. The mournful blast of its horn folded into a booming thunderclap.

The storm was directly overhead now and blinding sheets of

rain made the trestle slippery. The wind was so wild, raindrops skewed sideways. Ray slowed his pace to allow Skeeter to catch up with him. Larry was in the lead when Ray and Skeeter passed the halfway point. Bud trailed, but not by much. The group remained oblivious to the freight train as it gained on them.

A vibration on the track caused Ray to glance behind him.

"Train!" he screamed into the wind. His eyes were wide with fright.

Larry stopped, then looked back at the train with a terrified look on his face and his mouth open in a silent scream. He heard the blast of the train horn. He became immobile, unable to move forward or backward.

"Get off the tracks, Larry!" Ray screamed, while adjusting his load and hustling panic-stricken down the tracks. Bud caught up to them. His entire body was shaking with fear. Skeeter fell back. She was as white as a ghost. Her boots were soaked and dragging her down.

Larry quickly turned and started limping as fast as he could to get off the tracks. Ray glanced behind him to check the advance of the speeding two-story freight train behind him. It was almost hidden behind the veil of pelting rain. He wiped the rain from his eyes, startled to see it was coming too fast. He thought his heart would stop. They couldn't outrun it. The whistle sounded again, pleading with them to run faster.

Ray knew immediately the only chance they had of beating the train was the metal gangplank behind them. He grabbed Skeeter's arm at a dead run, and spun her around. Now the wind pushed them in the other direction and the rain almost closed their eyes. She kicked off the boots. Together they ran toward the behemoth, not from it, and it multiplied in size in seconds until it was as big as the sky. Bud followed them, head down, running blind.

Smoke poured out of the train's stack and down the sides of

the train, blowing fumes. Sucking the air. The vicious wind intent on knocking them off the tracks. Shards of rain, squalls of dirt and water throttled them. Kicked up from the speeding train. The air was on fire. The freight train was on them, blaring its horn, again and again. Thunderous rain spat at them. Ray felt the hot breath of the engine roaring down on them.

At the last possible second, he pushed Skeeter onto the gangplank and grabbed a girder. The pressure blast from the passing train viciously ripped his left arm from the girder and threw him onto metal wires strung between the girders and along the gangplank. The noise was deafening. He shut his eyes tight until the train tired of hurling debris and sped by in a huff of smoke.

The hard rain was swept away by the train, but the wind was still raw with an undercurrent that made the bridge unbalanced. One hundred feet beneath him, he saw the rolling waters of the Altamaha River. It was suddenly so quiet, he thought for a moment he was deaf.

Bud was curled up and motionless on the gangplank. Skeeter was lying on the platform, one skinny arm around a tie line, perilously close to falling. He squirmed back onto the safety of the gangplank and with his right hand, he grabbed Skeeter's arm just as she began to slide over the edge.

"Help me, Bud!" he screamed at him. Ray's left arm hung useless and bleeding at his side.

Bud stayed curled up on the gangplank.

"Help me, Ray," Skeeter cried.

Ray used all the strength in his right arm to hold onto her, but her arm was wet and slippery.

"I'm falling," she screamed.

"No, you're not," he shouted, even as his grip failed and he felt her slipping away. His right hand lost leverage as he tried in vain to hold on. In a trance, he felt his fingers slide away from Skeeter's arm, allowing her to fly for a time. When her body hit the water, Ray flinched in pain. At that moment, part of him died with her. She was pulled under the fast water.

Bud stood behind him.

Ray screamed into the wind. "It's my fault. I couldn't hang on." He watched the current carry Skeeter downriver. Tears stung his eyes. He collapsed onto the bridge, under the weight of Skeeter's death, and the pain in his mangled arm. Deep bloody cuts revealed muscle and bone. Larry helped him to his feet, took off his own shirt, and wrapped it carefully around Ray's arm and body to hold the left arm in place. "You did the best you could," Larry told him. "You saved the rest of us."

Larry grabbed Ray's backpack, as well as his, and helped him down the railroad tracks. Bud picked up what was left of Skeeter's big boots along with his backpack, then dragged them down the wet tracks.

Ray turned to stare at the bridge and the river, wiping away tears. "We'll never talk about this again," he told them. They understood and nodded in agreement, aware that nothing would be the same again.

The thunderstorm had moved on, and patches of blue sky peered through the clouds. A mist hung over the railroad trestle as the three young men walked away from the Altamaha River.

Chapter 19
Fishing
Thursday

"Ugh. That's awful," Ella said, "falling off a bridge to your death." Jackson Lee had just told her about the girl who fell from the bridge years ago.

"They didn't know there was a train coming," he explained. He cast his line out as far as possible, then tightened it up.

Grabbing a slip bobber, she tied her line on, then wound a large night crawler through the hook. "Sorry fella. I hope you can swim." With that caution, she raised the rod and tossed the line out as far she could into the current of the river. The bobber straightened up and wobbled as far as it could against the line, then tipped into the current. She sat down on a blanket to watch the river run by. Walter had already found a cushy spot under a mossy Cypress tree.

"Did I tell you the Cubs dropped a doubleheader to Milwaukee yesterday?"

"No," Jackson Lee said, casting his line out again. "Aren't they battling Pittsburgh for last place?" He was standing downhill from her.

"Funny," she retorted. "They're not dead yet." She saw him smiling under the brim of his hat. "All they need are a few left-handed pitchers under the age of forty."

She loved to fish, bobber fishing being her favorite. At the moment, Jackson Lee was concentrating on tying an iridescent plastic lure on his line.

"Hoping to catch a plastic fish?"

"Oddly enough, fish are crazy about this lure. A word of caution, though. When I bought the bait, a guy there said that the fish were biting so hard, you have to stand behind a tree to bait your hook." He smiled up at her, and winked.

She laughed with him. "Well, then you're taking your life in your hands here, standing out in the open like that."

Satisfied with his efforts, he cast the lure out, then reeled the line back just a little to tighten it up. The current grabbed it and held it midstream. "Do you need any help?"

She checked her bobber, bending to the right in the current. "No, I'm good."

There was a comfortable quietness between them. The day was very warm but the air had yet to achieve the summer humidity Georgia was known for. A breeze held the mosquitos at bay, at least for now, and the entire world seemed to be in repose. She closed her eyes and pictured the two of them as they were now, in this moment, fishing on the bank of the Altamaha River practically under the old railroad trestle bridge.

Jackson Lee wore long pants and a t-shirt, instead of his impeccably tailored suit, which would have been a little out of place. Like Ella, he wore a baseball cap, but with the Atlanta Braves logo, the bill stained from years of use. He pulled it down to the top of his glasses to shade his eyes and hide his smile. She liked to look at him when he didn't know it.

"Uh, I think you've got a bite there, Ella," he said.

"No, I don't." She didn't bother to open her eyes.

"I disagree. Your bobber has disappeared."

"Ridiculous." She sat up and reeled in her line. "I never catch anything."

To her surprise, a tiny perch had caught its lip on the hook, and just as it breeched the water, it fell free and swam away.

"Good."

He looked surprised. "You do understand the concept of fishing, don't you?"

She laughed. "To me, fishing is sitting by the river and letting my mind go free. While my night crawler disintegrates in the water. Sometimes I fish without any bait at all," she whispered loudly.

"You know," he said, with a grin and casting his line out again, "you don't have to pretend to fish. You can just sit there and enjoy the day."

"But I love to fish." Even to her, this sounded funny.

He smiled back, and reeled his line in. He set his pole down between two rocks and chose a spot on the blanket to sit down next to her.

"I think I'm done fishing," he said. "I'd rather spend the time with you."

He really was charming. She had enjoyed supper the night before, especially dancing with him. And kissing him. She had never been kissed like that before, with such obvious passion.

He picked up a small stick seemingly intent on uncovering pebbles and assembling them into groups based on size.

She reeled in her bobber, ending all pretense of fishing. "I guess the fish just aren't biting, huh?"

"No." He seemed distracted.

Walter chose that moment to bustle off into the woods. "Do you think I should stop him?" she asked. Spending all her life dog-less, she wasn't sure if dogs walked off and just kept walking, or returned on their own.

"He'll be back. We're his ride home," he assured her.

She hoped he was right. She had become fond of the little vagabond. "If I haven't told you yet, supper last night was amazing. I am not a cook. I just don't have the talent for it."

"No problem. I'm a great cook," he countered. "It would be a good reason to keep me around." He smiled at her.

"You can always cook for me, baby," she said with a sexy smile. "And thanks for helping me figure stuff out. I usually depend on Walter as a sounding board, and believe me, he is a great listener. But his feedback leaves a lot to be desired. He only has two expressions—disappointment and utter disgust."

He laughed. "You know he's a dog, right?"

They heard him howl. "Squirrel," she said.

Jackson Lee handed Ella a cold bottle of water from the cooler. "Would you like a sandwich?"

She twisted the cap off and drank almost all of it. "Delicious. No, I'm not hungry yet." He closed the lid, and sat down next to her. Ella held his hand, intertwining his big fingers with her small ones. They watched the river, insistent in its travel, and always sure of where to go.

"What time are you leaving for the airport?" An uncomfortable topic.

"Probably around noon," she answered. "In a couple of hours." She gave him his hand back because hers was sweaty. "I don't want to talk about it." She could almost feel the small town holding her back from leaving.

"I'm going to miss you." He didn't smile, he took her hand again.

"Me, too. I admit that I'm smitten," she said, shyly. In every way.

He laughed. "Smitten?"

"Yes," she said, and explained. "You have bewitched me, cast a spell on me. Do those words help?"

He breathed a deep sigh, and smiled. "I'm crazy about you, too."

His eyes were barely visible below the bill of his cap, but they lit up his face. Ella carefully removed his hat and his glasses. Then she took her hat and sunglasses off. She kissed him softly on the lips. "I didn't want to fog up your glasses again."

He kissed her neck, then whispered in her ear. "I love long, slow kisses that last an eternity." He lifted her chin and kissed her lips. "The small of a woman's back, and the cool, softness of her cheek." He nuzzled her neck and she quivered. He gently kissed her lips, exploring her mouth with his, his hand on the back of her head. His kisses became more urgent.

In the woods, Walter was howling again. It definitely wasn't his squirrel howl, or his disappointment howl. It was a howl that meant something. They both stopped and listened.

Chapter 20
What Walter found in the river
Thursday

Ella slipped quickly into police detective mode as soon as she saw the body, caught on a huge tree branch that kept it from floating farther downriver. Walter had stopped howling, lost interest, and wandered off to examine something under a dead branch. She waved Jackson Lee back from the scene.

"Call Walter and put on his leash. You both have to stay away from the crime scene," she shouted. He waved back in acknowledgment. It was vital to secure the scene until it was thoroughly investigated. She pulled her phone from her pocket and called Chief Jones.

"Detective Flynn here, Chief. We've discovered a body in the river, on the shore of the Altamaha River, down by the bridge."

"Okay, Flynn," he said hurriedly. "We're on it."

"Thanks, Chief. I've secured the scene. See you soon." She imagined she could hear the squeal of squad car tires leaving the station.

When she cautiously crept closer, she saw that the body in the river was floating face down. Bloating forced the clothing to tightly bind the abdomen, distorting the body's physical appearance. She couldn't tell from this angle if it was male or female. The pink top suggested it was female.

The body was snagged on the limbs of a dead tree, fastened to the shore by a myriad of dry and brittle interlocking branches. It was going to be difficult to remove it from the river. But before it reached that point, they would have to figure out if the body was dumped in the river right here, or if it floated downriver from a different location. That would be up to the Crime Scene Investigator, or whoever the Georgia Bureau of Investigation sent to the crime scene, to sift through the evidence and photos and arrive at a conclusion. From the shore, it appeared to her that the body could be attached to something like a weight, possibly, to prevent it from floating up, or maybe to hold it in one place.

In Chicago, bodies found in the Little Calumet or Chicago River were harbingers of spring. In mid-March or April when the snow and ice melted, they would pop up along the shore or float by stuck to something, like this one. She had seen a lot of them in eight years.

It could be a drowning. Maybe the person fell out of a boat while fishing, or swimming. Or, the body could have been deposited in the river after death. If the autopsy found water in the lungs, it was a drowning. Time would tell. She scanned the ground for any type of physical evidence, like footprints. It had rained hard Tuesday night and may have washed any prints away.

Minutes later, the Chief and Sgt. Bobby Dean arrived and took charge of the crime scene. Jackson Lee stood off in the trees with Walter, who had started howling like his little legs were being pulled off. She waved to the Chief, then walked over to them to quiet Walter. He wagged his tail and stopped. It was magical when he wasn't howling.

She sat in the grass and kissed the dog on his snout. "Thanks, buddy. Most dogs can't find a body in a river, but I guess you're good at everything." She turned to Jackson Lee, who joined her on the little hill. "This is not at all what I expected to happen today," she told him, then smiled. "I would rather be spending my time with you, but this is really important." He smiled back.

"Two dead bodies, found three days apart. Coincidence?" she asked him.

He stroked his beard in thought. "Dead people in Prosper aren't usually found in the river, or suffocated in their homes. I suppose it could be coincidence, but it's likely not."

"Yeah," she agreed. "When the body is identified, I'd like to find out what kind of connection they had to my father. If any."

"When will they do the autopsy?"

"Today, for sure. I know that bodies in rivers decompose slower because the water is cold, and the current helps delay it, too. But once they take it out of the river, they'd better haul ass to Savannah because decomposition will make up for lost time." She was sure he had seen the effects of decomposition many times when he prepared a body for burial.

She thought about the body in the river. "I'm really interested in who this is, and how long they've been in the river. The day the body was dumped in the river would tell us a lot."

The Coroner had arrived on scene and was talking to Chief Jones.

She patted Walter on the head as he curled up next to her. "I'd appreciate it if you'd take my little buddy home," she said. "It's going to take a while to get the scene processed and the body hauled away to the GBI Crime Lab, then I'll have to fill out a report at the police department since I found the body." He looked disappointed, she pretended she didn't notice.

"I know technically Walter found the body, but he is a known felon and they won't believe a word he howls."

Not even a chuckle. "I can come back later," he offered.

She gave him a thin smile. "Not necessary. I'll get a ride back with one of the guys, I'm sure. By then maybe they'll have come up with an identification."

"What about your flight back to Chicago?" He tilted his head when he glanced at her.

"Right. I forgot about that. I guess I got carried away. I'm probably going to miss it."

"Your Chief isn't going to like that, right?"

"I'm sure he won't, but I'll call him later and tell him what's going on." She smiled at him. "No problem."

"All right then," he said, kissing her on the cheek. "Call me when you can."

"Absolutely." The truth was Chief Warner would not be happy about this, and she would be in big trouble. "Everything will be just fine," she said.

Walter shuffled off with his companion, and she returned to the scene of the crime which had become quite active.

She sought out the Coroner and introduced herself. "Detective Flynn, Sir. Are you the person who called me the other day to tell me about my father?"

"I am the same," he said, smiling. "I'm the Coroner from Wayne County, Elmer Berry."

Under the large brim of his white canvas hat, his big nose was raspberry-colored, and matched his bloodshot eyes. "Thanks for everything you did for my father. It was a good idea to have his body autopsied."

"You're welcome, detective, but I'm very sorry how it turned out. Homicide was not the manner of death anybody wanted." He was a compact man, seemingly tall when placed on a low hill, when in actuality, he was shorter than Ella. She pegged him for the kind of guy who would put lifts in his shoes.

"What time did you find the body?" Chief Jones asked, pulling her away from the Coroner.

"It was before ten o'clock this morning. I'd say nine-fifty." Chief Jones wrote it down in his notebook. "How did you find it?"

"Walter found the body. Jackson Lee and I were fishing about one hundred yards away, practically under the bridge, when he wandered off. I heard him howl his 'what the heck is this' howl, which is very different from his squirrel howl."

Chief Jones didn't say anything, just looked at her.

"We ran to find him, and there he was at the shoreline, complaining about the body in the river."

"Complaining?"

She smiled at the Chief. He looked confused. "It's hard to tell if Walter is pissed off, disappointed, or just plain aggravated. That's why he has different howls." She acted like that explained everything.

The Chief nodded. "The dog found the body in the river."

"Yes, sir," she said. "I secured the scene and called you right away."

"I appreciate that, Flynn. Did you notice anyone else in this area today?"

She chewed on her bottom lip. "No, sir. I didn't see anybody from the time we got here until we found the body."

The Crime Scene Specialist from the Georgia Bureau of Investigation had arrived, and he was busy laying a yellow line border around the crime scene to begin gathering evidence. Several cameras were in a large metal box, along with evidence bags and other necessary items.

It was getting quite crowded with the arrival of Mayor Wheeler and Officer Connie. The Mayor was talking and posturing for his constituents, wherever they might be. He was not impressive, and she was not impressed.

"Hey, girl," Connie said. "Found another dead body for us. Thanks a lot."

"I heard your ginormous bike pull up. It's SO loud."

Connie smiled with obvious pride. "Yeah, baby, it's a monster, and I love it!"

Ella continued answering her question. "Technically, Walter found the body. He's a forensic anthropologist in his spare time."

That made Connie laugh. "I saw you and Jackson Lee over there."

Ella knew she had. Avoiding the obvious question, she explained that Walter needed to be taken home. He had no concept of crime scenes or personal space.

"Do you know the Crime Scene Specialist? Can you introduce me?"

"I do," she said. They stood at the edge of the yellow tape. "Moses," Connie said to get his attention, "This here is Detective Ella Flynn from Chicago. She found the body."

Moses had been photographing the body as it clung to the tree branches in the river. He smiled in her direction. "Pleasure, ma'am." He tipped his GBI hat.

She smiled back at him. "Thanks for the introduction, Connie. Looks like we'll be here for a while."

Chief Jones walked up. "You know you don't need to be here, Flynn. You can stop by the department later and we'll take your statement."

She had been trying to be unobtrusive, hoping her presence would be overlooked. "I'd like to stay if I can, Chief," she said, quickly changing the subject. "Do you have any idea of who this might be?"

He was cooperative. "We're checking around for people who've gone missing lately. It's a little hard to tell until we autopsy the body." The Mayor called him over, and Ella breathed a sigh of relief when he left.

Connie's eyebrows furrowed in thought. "Why do you want to stay?"

She told her the truth. "I'm interested. I want to know who it is. And I don't have anything else to do since you have my father's killer locked up." They might have wrapped up their investigation, but Ella hadn't. This death could be related to her father's death.

"Okay. Try to blend in."

"Thanks for the tip." She walked to an area outside of the crime scene and watched Moses measure the area and tie grid lines to examine each inch of ground. He was thorough. No bullet shells, no footprints. The rain seemed to have removed all trace evidence.

Connie left for the police station in a loud rumble that practically shook the earth and knocked birds out of the sky. The GBI Medical Examiner arrived, but it wasn't Loretta Mae Montgomery this time. She was disappointed. Loretta Mae would have been someone to talk with.

Several GBI agents arrived to help with the process. It was becoming standing-room-only. She moved even farther to the outskirts of the crime scene, out of the way, and started scrolling through her phone messages. It was two hours later when the body was ready to be removed from the water.

The Coroner supervised the procedure from the shore. When they extricated the body from the labyrinth of elements holding it in place, they turned it over. Ella was surprised at how young the woman was. Her body was swollen from her time in the river, but still recognizable. She wore shorts, but the remaining fabric cut into her water-logged skin. A pink top was wrapped around her leg. Other than what looked like a bullet hole in her forehead, there weren't any obvious wounds, but it would be hard to see them at this stage of the investigation, and they could have happened post-mortem in the river. They'd have to wait for the autopsy later today.

She watched them load the body in the ambulance and head north to Savannah. Ella caught a ride back to the police station with the Coroner.

Chapter 21
Police Department
Thursday

Ella couldn't wait to take a shower and wash off the acrid scent of death. This body was not her first. She'd seen dead people who exploded, were run over, shot, sliced, stabbed, and even exhumed. But this particular dead body had recently been a living, breathing young woman, before she was found in the river with a bullet hole in her forehead. Someone was responsible for taking her life and tossing her in the river. No matter how many dead bodies she saw, each one bothered her on some level. She would never be numb to it.

In less than an hour, she was back at police headquarters. Minus Big Dick Wheeler, the cast was the same. Chief Jones was meeting with his staff of two, and Jackson Lee and Walter trailed in right behind her.

He was dressed better than her, as usual, wearing khaki slacks that fit him perfectly, with a white shirt that showed off his summer tan and his well-muscled arms. Ella was decked out in acid-washed blue jeans, Christmas socks, Converse high-tops, a pink hoodie, and a Cubs baseball hat. Her long hair was clean and brushed, as were her teeth. They sat down next to each other at an empty desk.

When the Chief turned in their direction, she asked: "Any new information?"

"We have a tentative identification, based on a picture, of a young girl who went missing last week in Jessup." He handed the picture to her.

Even with bloating and decomposition, it resembled the girl in the river. "We're just waiting on dental records. The fish had nibbled her fingertips, so no fingerprints."

"Understandable," she agreed. "What's her name?"

"Mary Ellen Bellacourt," he read from a paper on his desk. "She was sixteen. She ran away so many times, her mother didn't even report it this time." She could tell it bothered the Chief that she was a runaway. He would have tried to fix her.

"She lived in Jessup?"

"A little north of Jessup, in an unincorporated area."

Connie piped up from the next desk. "Chief, didn't you tell me she was pregnant?" Just Connie being helpful. Ella smiled at her, and she smiled back.

"Oh, yeah," he confirmed. "Eight weeks pregnant." He frowned. "Such a tragedy."

"I'm sorry. That's awful. Is there a manner of death, yet?"

The Chief glanced in her direction. "There was a bullet hole in her forehead, so we're going with homicide."

"Good choice," she said. It had turned out to be a really nasty crime. A young girl, pregnant, shot in the head, and thrown in the river. It didn't get much worse than that. Not even in Chicago.

"Why don't you fill out your statement, Flynn." It was a rhetorical question. He had a quizzical look on his face. "Weren't you supposed to leave today? It's already five o'clock."

She was busy organizing her summary of the crime. "Missed my flight. I'll leave tomorrow," she said, dismissing his question.

"All right, then," he said.

"I know it's early, but do you have any suspects?" Jackson Lee asked.

"Yeah, we do," the Chief said. "The girl was going out with Junior

Wheeler, so we're going to start there.

"The Mayor had a problem with Junior going out with Mary Ellen," Connie said. "He made a big deal out of wanting Junior to break up with her."

"Did Junior know she was pregnant?" she asked the Chief.

"This is what I plan to find out, Flynn. I'm going to talk to him tomorrow."

Ella had finished writing her statement and needed a beer desperately. "Okay, Chief. I'll take Walter here, and go home." She grabbed the end of his leash. Turning to Jackson Lee, she said: "If you're up for it, and you don't have to work tonight, why don't you come over to the blue house around seven, and I'll make supper. Hot dogs and beer."

He grinned. "That sounds great. Do you want me to bring a bottle of wine?"

Ella shook her head, no. "Wine makes me too passionate."

He laughed. "There is no such thing as too passionate. But we could definitely do a study on it, if you want."

"Okay, I like that idea. Let's see how I react to beer."

"I am very interested in the results," he said, kissing her cheek, then kissing her lips.

"Get a room," Connie said, smiling. "No PDAs in the police department."

They both laughed, and left the building.

Chapter 22
The Mayor has a Bad Day
Thursday

The Mayor's Office

Mayor Big Dick Wheeler was pacing back and forth between the two windows in his office. He was furious. The object of his anger, Junior, sat in a chair in front of his desk, and appeared to be studying something on the carpet.

"When was the last time you saw Mary Ellen? He walked a little faster. "When was the last time you talked to her?" He was talking faster, too.

"Sunday. I picked her up and we went to Roxie's

Big Dick sat down at his desk, glaring at his son. "You might as well tell me what happened. She was shot in the head. Did you fight with her?"

Junior was taken aback by his father's assumption that he committed the crime. "No, sir," he said, loudly. "I didn't do it."

Big Dick stopped walking. "Really? Where's your gun. I want it now."

Junior twisted around and took a Sig Sauer handgun from his belly band. He handed it to his father.

The Mayor sniffed the barrel. "When did you fire this last, boy?"

He was evasive. "I don't remember."

"It smells like it was fired recently." He handed the gun back to Junior. "As soon as you leave here, clean it good so it smells like oil. They're gonna take your gun, boy."

"Yes, sir," he said, sliding the gun back into the belly band.

Big Dick stood directly in front of Junior. "Listen to me, son. This is very important. She never told us she was pregnant. Understand? You had no idea."

"Yes, sir," he said. "But why is that important?"

The Mayor smiled a sly smile. "That's your motive. She told you she was pregnant, wanted money, and you killed her and tossed her body in the river."

"But I didn't do that. I didn't. You believe me, don't you?"

Big Dick finally sat down. "It don't matter if I believe you or not. Your gun is clean and you didn't know she was pregnant. You had no motive to kill her."

"I get it," he said. "But I still didn't do it." He looked offended.

"Chief Jones is going to call you into the police station real soon, so be prepared. Now get out of here and clean that gun."

After Junior left, the Mayor sat at his desk staring out the window until it was time for supper. It was up to Junior now. If he could hold it together. Time would tell. He honestly didn't know what to believe.

Chapter 23
Parts of the Puzzle
Thursday night

Ella met Jackson Lee at the door, put her arms around his neck, and kissed him hard. If he was surprised, he didn't act like it.

"Is that hot dogs I smell, boiling on the stove?" He sniffed the air.

"Ballpark franks, so they should taste a lot like a baseball field." She turned off the single burner that worked. "How long are you supposed to cook these things?"

He looked at the pinkish-gray hot dogs in the pan, split open. "They're done," he said.

"Good. I wasn't sure if they were pre-cooked or not, so I've been boiling them for a while."

"Beer?" she asked, taking a cold one from the refrigerator and handing it to him. "And as a special treat," she said, smiling, "I have hot dog buns."

"Catsup?"

She furrowed her brows. "You don't put catsup on a hot dog in Chicago. Mustard, onions, pickles. Possibly chili. These are Chicago hot dogs."

"I see," he said, smiling. "I'll just cover it up with some mustard then."

Ella prepared the entree on paper plates, and cut one up for Walter. The garnish was pickles from the back of the refrigerator. She was of the opinion that expiration dates were a marketing strategy, so she didn't even check. Along with the discovery of a bag of Cheetos, there was beer.

It didn't take long to eat supper, and Jackson Lee cleaned up by tossing the paper plates and napkins in the trash. He popped the top on a new beer. "So, what's up with the investigation? Anything new?" All three of them sat on the sofa.

"The Medical Examiner just confirmed Mary Ellen was submerged in the river Sunday afternoon sometime. She was already dead when she went into the river because there was no water in her lungs. A nine-mm bullet passed through her forehead. Cause of death. The person, or persons, who brought her body to the river were probably counting on the current floating her downriver, far away from Prosper."

Walter panted and started to whine. When she stroked his back, he stopped whining and came as close to a smile as he could, which wasn't that close.

"The M.E. also confirmed where we found her, was also where she was dropped off."

Walter hopped off the sofa and lay down on a rug.

Ella went to the refrigerator, grabbed two cans of beer, and tossed one to Jackson Lee.

She sat back down on the sofa and drank the beer a little too quickly. She felt like burping, but didn't. Because she was a lady. Jackson Lee went to the refrigerator for more, but she waved him off. "I think I'd better hold off for now." He laughed when she tossed her can, and missed the recycle bin.

Jackson Lee sat back down. He was silent, busy wiping the dog hair from his clothes.

It was frustrating. "Without finding Larry, I'll never be sure who killed my father. I wish I had more time, but I really have to leave tomorrow. And this time I mean it." She smiled. "I hate that I can't finish this."

"You only had two days. It just wasn't enough time."

"Thanks, Buddy," she said to Jackson Lee. "You've been a huge help." She kissed him on the cheek. "You're a peach." She lay down on her side on the sofa with her head in his lap. He stroked her long hair. "I feel so overwhelmed."

"I don't think anybody expected you to solve these crimes. You're putting a lot of pressure on yourself." He rubbed her back.

"Thank you for listening to me," she said, enjoying the back rub. "I know sometimes I sound deranged, but my intuition tells me it isn't as obvious as it appears."

"Has your intuition been wrong before?" he asked.

"Shit, all the time." She laughed. "I won't drag this out forever, I promise."

"I will always listen to you. Now it's your turn to listen to me. I know you wanted more information on your father, and I found out something that I think you should know."

She sat up, interested. "What?"

He adjusted his glasses. "Earlier today, I was telling you about the girl who fell off the bridge years ago. I got to thinking about it, so I searched around in the online archives of the Wayne County Examiner for some information."

"Go on. I'm definitely interested."

"I had to go back to 1985, June fourth. There were four kids crossing the Railroad Trestle Bridge coming back from the other side of the river, when a freight train came down the tracks."

"Oh my gosh," she said. "I would have panicked."

He nodded his head. "The thing about the bridge is, it isn't very wide, and when a train comes, it takes up the entire width of the bridge.

If you're in the way, there is nowhere to go and you can't get off the bridge."

"Didn't they know that?" It seemed like it should be common knowledge.

"They probably did know it. But trains can come down the tracks anytime. Sometimes once a day, sometimes not for a week. There never has been a schedule."

"I see, it was just bad luck then. Does this story have anything to do with my father?" She was wondering what the point was.

"It has a lot to do with your father." He licked his lips, and continued. "Ray Flynn was one of the kids on the bridge."

"What?" She did a quick calculation in her head. "He must have just graduated from high school in 1985."

"He did. He had two friends with him. A guy with a gimpy leg named Larry, and another named Bud Santos. You probably know him better as Father Santos, the Priest at the catholic church."

It took a few minutes for all of it to sink in. "What about the girl who fell into the river and died?"

"Her name was Skeeter. I guess she was just hiking with them. There was a metal gangplank off the bridge, about halfway down, and they jumped on it to escape the train. Your father's arm was practically torn off by the pressure from the train passing by, and the young girl was unable to hold on. She fell to her death."

It was a lot of information to process. "Thanks, I really appreciate this. The Larry on the bridge is my Larry-with-a-limp. And Father Santos was a childhood friend of my father."

"That's it in a nutshell," he said. "The injury your father took to his arm, along with the death of the young girl, probably had a big impact on him. I don't know for sure, but the trauma could have influenced his drinking. It might also have had something to do with the reason he couldn't stay with you and your mother. He may have felt he didn't deserve that life."

"We'll never know," she said, "but it must have been hard for him to live with what happened." She glanced at him. "I feel really bad for him."

He smiled at her. "I do, too, but I think it explains a lot."

She smiled back. "I've learned so much in just a couple of days. My perspective on everything in my world has changed."

"Like what?"

"Like I thought Chicago was the best city in the world, until I came here. And I thought my father didn't even remember me. That was wrong." She grabbed his hand. "I even thought I knew what love was. I was wrong about that, too."

He squeezed her hand. "I know you have to go back. But I really hope you come back to Prosper. Come back to me."

"I'd like to," she said. "But right now, I have to straighten some things out back home."

He stood up and offered her his hand. "You look tired. It's time for me to go." She stood up.

"You're right. It has been a long day and I'm so tired."

This time when they reached the door, it was his turn. He cupped her face in his hands, kissing her softly and longingly. Ella was breathless. *Whew*, she thought. *Wow*.

"Thanks for supper. It was interesting." He gave her a big smile and a thumbs up.

"Thanks for eating it. I'll see you before I leave for Atlanta tomorrow. She waved goodbye as he walked down the sidewalk. She definitely wanted to wrap up the investigations, but she definitely did not want to leave Jackson Lee.

Chapter 24
Time to go
Friday morning

When Ella realized it was a phone call from Chief Warner, she froze. She should have called him first.

"Flynn," he said. "We expected you back yesterday. What's going on?" He sounded angry, his usual loud, demanding tone. She turned the volume down on her phone so his voice wouldn't echo in the room.

"Hi Chief," she said. "How are you?" She didn't wait for a response. "Yes, I had a flight back planned," she lied, "but a body was found in the river yesterday. I thought it could be connected to my father's death." It seemed ridiculous when she said it out loud.

Silence. "I don't even want to know how you came to that conclusion, Flynn. You were due back yesterday from a two-day bereavement leave. That is a feeble excuse." If possible, his voice was even more strident, she was glad they were separated by hundreds of miles. "What do the local police think about it?" He was going to be awfully hard to please.

"They think maybe it's a separate case." She had to be honest, in case he called Chief Jones to better understand what was going on. "They arrested a residential burglar for my father's homicide." *Honesty sucks.*

She heard him groan and take a deep breath. "I expect you back today, by First Watch, eleven p.m. No more excuses. Are we clear on that?"

"Crystal. I'll be there tonight, Chief." She was glad he didn't say "or else" before he ended the call.

Her mind immediately turned to Jackson Lee. He was a tough guy to leave behind. Being with him the last few days had been a new experience for her, he was so different from anyone she knew.

"Walter?" He had been napping on the sofa, and he opened his eyes. "You're having breakfast at the Funeral Home this morning. Grab your leash, buddy." He put his head down and went back to sleep while Ella threw her suitcase in her car and tidied up the house. He eventually became interested in what she was doing, slid off the sofa, and joined her.

"Don't ever forget I love you, Walter," she said softly, kissing him on the nose. He snorted and sneezed. She was sure it was a sign of respect.

Outside the little blue bungalow, the sun was halfway up. Except for a dog barking faraway in the distance, it was quiet. Prosper was so different from Chicago. Ella lifted up Walter's ass and boosted him into the car. He liked to ride shotgun in the front seat, so she let him, and drove to the Armstrong Funeral Home.

Chapter 25
Saying Goodbye
Friday Morning

Martha answered Ella's knock on the front door and went to find Jackson Lee. She stood with Walter in the foyer. The flowers in the vases were fresh. They helped make it a little less somber inside, but in no way did they make her feel better about leaving.

When he saw her, he smiled. She smiled back. His face changed quickly to a frown when he saw Walter, and remembered she was on her way back to Chicago. "You're leaving then."

She nodded. "I have to." She unhooked Walter's leash, and handed it to him. "Chief Warner called me this morning and gave me an ultimatum. He wants me back today, by First Watch, tonight."

He crossed his arms over his chest, and nodded. "Of course, then, you have to go. I understand." He breathed deeply and sighed. "I knew this would happen, but it still makes me sad." He was close enough to touch, but felt miles away. Ella had to glance away for a second.

"We only had a couple of days," she said. "It wasn't enough."

He stepped closer and gently held her face in his hands. "They were the best days of my life," he said, and kissed her. She couldn't resist him. She put her arms around his neck and kissed him back like she would never see him again.

She pulled back and smiled. "My best days, too." His eyes were lighter in color in the sunlight, with flecks of gold and azure, like the color of the sky on a clear day. "Your eyes are beautiful," she told him. Rather than hiding his eyes, his glasses served to emphasize them.

He took her hand and walked her out to the porch swing. They rocked for a while in silence, holding hands, shoulder to shoulder. Mid-morning in Prosper was peaceful. The cars that passed by were noiseless, and even the birds were mute.

"Without Larry, I can't solve this case," she said, as if a question had been asked. "Maybe Bobby Dean was right. It could have been the burglar, even if my father saw something that scared him. It still could have been the burglar that killed him." She studied his face for an answer.

He nodded his head in agreement. "Yes, that could have been what happened." He turned to her. "Are you going to accept that? Is the investigation closed?"

She tugged her earlobe, pondering the question. "I might. Maybe getting some distance on the whole thing will help."

"You mean from Chicago?" He had always been the voice of reason to Ella's complex theories.

"Yes, I think that's what I mean. Maybe I'm too close to the crime. Maybe the solution is simple and I've made it complicated."

They slowly rocked in silence again. "What happens now?" he asked, his attention focused on her.

She rubbed her hands back and forth on her thighs. "I'm going to stop and say goodbye to Connie and the Chief, then off to Atlanta, drop off the car, and fly back to Chicago in time for my shift.

"Come back, okay?" He was serious. "Is it all right if I call you?" He seemed hesitant to ask.

"Yes, please call me. I can't imagine not talking to you." She smiled at him.

He smiled back. "I'll do that."

"Good," she said, and stood up to go. He joined her and hugged her tight. Walter howled inside the house.

"That's his breakfast howl. I told him he was eating here."

"Okay," he said. "I know that you have to go." He smiled.

"I think this is the hardest thing I've ever had to do," she told him. Then she turned and walked to her car. She waved goodbye with a smile, but it was a lie.

Chapter 26
Connie
Friday Morning

"Hey, Connie," Ella asked when she walked in. "Is the Chief in?"

"Hey, girl. He's not here yet." She hadn't stopped typing to answer, hadn't looked up from her desk.

"Oh. I wanted to say goodbye to him. I'm on my way to Atlanta right now, to catch a flight to Chicago." She was disappointed. She wanted to tell him she'd considered what he said about contacting her father, and agreed with him. He was right. There was a lot she could have done to reach out to him before he died, and now it was too late. She would accept her part in their estrangement. She didn't want to be adult about it, but it seemed like the thing to do.

Connie stopped typing and glanced her way. "Right now? That sucks. I'm gonna miss you." She stood up to give Ella a hug. She squeezed her tight.

"Me, too," she said. "Is it okay if I call you to find out what's going on?"

"Absolutely. Call me anytime." She had been a good friend to her, and Connie would keep her informed, too.

"Is the Chief still going to interview Junior today?" She knew he was.

Connie was fully engaged now, leaning her hip against a desk. "He sure is. Junior looks guilty as hell, but it's all circumstantial, so far."

"The Chief seems to know what he's doing." *I don't want to leave. I want to be part of the investigation,* she thought, but hesitated to say it out loud.

"I've got confidence in him," she agreed. She studied Ella's face. "What about Jackson Lee? Are you just going to walk away from him?" She went directly to the heart.

Ella took a deep breath. "If I'm in Chicago and he's here, I don't see how it would work."

Connie pursed her lips and focused on her friend. "Your job is more important than he is. Is that what you're telling me?"

"It sounds pretty harsh when you say it like that," she said, frowning. "Tell me Connie, how long did you know Dixie before you became a couple?"

She shrugged her shoulder. "A while," she said.

"I bet it was longer than two or three days. Listen, Jackson Lee doesn't come with a guarantee." Connie was tuned in. "To me, he is the most exciting man I've ever known and I'm crazy about him. But I've only known him for a couple of days." Ella smiled, thinking of him, but it faded.

She nodded.

"I haven't known him long enough to know if he falls madly in love with every woman he meets, but it only lasts for a month or two. Or, if he is the real thing, and I'm the woman he's looking for." Connie seemed to understand. "The only way I can find out is to wait and see."

"I see what you mean."

"My Chief wants me back in Chicago today. Maybe when I look at Jackson Lee from a thousand miles away, I'll know what to do. I hope so."

"I just hope you won't regret leaving him. Some things come by only one time." Ella nodded in agreement. "Sometimes you have to jump in and see what happens."

She smiled at Connie. "I might change my mind," she said.

Connie sat back down at her desk and sorted through a few papers. Without looking at Ella, she said: "If you change your mind, I hope it's before he finds somebody else." Then she turned to her. "I wouldn't even have to think about it if it was my job, or Dixie. Dixie is my life. It's good to know the difference." She turned back to her work.

"Thanks for your advice," she said to the back of Connie's head. She sighed, and picked her keys back up. It was the beginning of a very long day that wouldn't end until tomorrow morning when she finished her shift.

She felt completely empty inside.

Chapter 27
The Interview #1
Friday

Chief Lovey Jones

Junior Wheeler strolled into the police station with a swagger that pissed off Chief Lovey Jones. Somebody being questioned about a murder investigation should be contrite. His body language displayed the wrong attitude.

He waited at the door to the Chief's office. "Hi, Chief. You want to talk to me?"

He didn't look up right away, made him wait. "Come in, Junior. Take a chair." He watched him walk in, nonchalant. Sit down. He was wearing a baseball cap. "Take the hat off," he told him. He did.

"Do you have your gun with you?"

"Yes, sir."

"Please hand it to me." The Chief held out his hand and took it, placing it in a drawer. "I'm recording this conversation. Say something like 'it's okay with me.'"

"Yes, sir. It's okay with me that you're recording." Junior shifted in his chair.

"Thanks. Now I'm going to ask you some questions." He watched Junior.

"Yes, sir," he said, crossing his legs, making himself comfortable.

The Chief didn't want that. "Put your legs down and sit up straight." He did. He looked like he had lost some of his confidence. That's what the Chief wanted.

"What's your name?"

"Richard Wheeler, Junior."

"How old are you?"

"Twenty."

"Where do you live?"

"On Somerset."

Chief Jones glanced up at him. "City?"

"Oh yeah, Prosper, Georgia."

"Cell phone number."

"408-776-4040."

"I think that's the basic stuff I need. We'll get on with the interview." The Chief sat back in his chair and scrutinized the young man in front of him. "How long have we known each other, Junior?"

"Since you came to Prosper, Chief. Four years, I guess." He was starting to fidget in his seat. His phone rang. He didn't answer it, turned it off and handed it the Chief.

"Thanks," he said, and put it in the drawer with the gun. "Do you know Mary Ellen Bellacourt?"

"Yes, sir, I do." He had a nervous smile, and he had started to tap his foot on the floor in a staccato rhythm.

"How long have you known her?" The Chief was pleased to see Junior displaying signs of anxiety. He was taking this seriously.

He scanned the ceiling for an answer. "About three months, maybe more."

"Are you aware Mary Ellen was only sixteen years old?" Sometimes teenage girls looked much older than their age. The Chief knew that.

"I never asked her how old she was. She wasn't in school," he said, as if it explained everything.

"She was sixteen," the Chief said again. "How did you meet her?"

Junior pursed his lips and thought about it. "I was hanging out with some guys at a party, and she was there. We hooked up."

"Tell me exactly what that means when you say, 'hooked up.'" It was too vague of a statement.

"Everybody was drinking, and she was, too. She came on to me, and we went out to my car. We had sex." He was trying to be polite about it. He smiled.

"Did you have unprotected sex?" This was a fairly important question.

"Sure. I figured she was taking care of it."

"Did you ask her?"

"There wasn't time." Junior smirked. The Chief liked him a little less every time he spoke.

"How often did you see her? Once a week, every day…"

"At first," Junior said, "every day. But then my dad found out we were going out, and told me to leave her alone. Then we had to sneak around."

"Why did your father want you to leave her alone?" The Chief thought he already knew the answer.

Junior squirmed in his chair. "He said she was a slut and she'd scam me outta everything I had."

That was definitely something Big Dick would say. "What did you think about that?"

"I liked her. She was funny and I was enjoying myself."

"I bet you were," the Chief said, with a knowing smile. No one would accuse Junior Wheeler of being good looking. He had more than a passing resemblance to Big Dick, who could be mistaken for a weasel.

His tiny eyes were set too close together. His nose was sharp where it should be flat. The mustache he was trying to grow had very few hairs, and they were only visible in a certain light. His thinness was changing to portly so that someday he could be egg-shaped, just like his dad.

Chief Jones decided Big Dick could be right about Mary Ellen. It's possible she was trying to hook a sugar daddy.

"When was the last time you saw Mary Ellen?"

Junior didn't hesitate. "Sunday. Last week. I picked her up at her house and we went to a bar."

"Which bar?"

"Roxie's in Jessup."

"What time did you get there?"

"It was after lunch. Probably one o'clock." He started tapping his foot again.

"How long did you stay?"

"About an hour. She said she was going to meet somebody, so I took her home."

"What time was that, when you got to her house."

"About two-thirty."

"You're sure that was the last time you saw her?"

He shrugged his shoulders. "Yeah, I said that, didn't I?"

"Don't get smart with me, boy," the Chief said. "If I feel like it, I'll ask you the same question a hundred times. Understand?" His eyes were narrow and dark.

Junior sat up a little straighter. "Yes, sir."

"Now tell me what you did after you dropped Mary Ellen off at her house.".

"I drove home and hung out there for the rest of the night. Ask my dad."

"Was your dad there with you?"

He looked at his feet. "I guess not. No, he wasn't there."

"Were you aware that the autopsy revealed Mary Ellen was eight weeks pregnant at the time of her death?" The big question of the day.

Junior looked surprised. "She was pregnant? I did not know that." He was a bad liar and the Chief could tell.

"Yes, she was. She never told you that?"

"Nope. This is the first I've heard of it."

"Another thing we found out is Mary Ellen was shot in the forehead, at close range, with a gun that shoots eight mm bullets. What type of bullets do you have in your gun?"

"Eight-millimeter, he said. "It's a Sig Sauer."

"Yes, I saw that," the Chief said. "We'll check your gun."

Junior's demeanor had changed from cocky to a sense of impending doom. He sat very still.

"Another thing we found out, Junior, is that Mary Ellen's body was dumped in the river sometime Sunday night. When was the last time you saw her?" He smiled at Junior.

"Sunday," he repeated.

The Chief sat back in his chair and focused on the young man in his office. "Do you have anything you'd like to tell me?"

He looked terrified. "No, sir."

"Think about it. Are you sure you don't want to tell me something?"

He looked like he might vomit. "No. I don't have anything to say."

"All right, then," Chief Jones said. "You're free to leave. But stick around Prosper in case we have more questions."

He stood up so fast his chair slid back to the wall with a thud. "Yes, sir," he said, and left the office.

The Chief turned off the recorder. It was all circumstantial right now. He'd have to talk to Mary Ellen's mother and find out what the girl did Sunday afternoon. It might all fall together.

He turned off the light in his office. "Good night, Connie," he said on his way out. He had to figure out what to make his wife for supper. He should probably stop by the store.

It was a quiet afternoon in Prosper.

Chapter 28
Back at work in Chicago
Friday night

Chicago

Chief Warner made a point of checking on Ella when her shift started. She would have been surprised if he didn't. They exchanged pleasantries, and he left.

"Glad to see you back, Flynn," Domzalski said. He smiled and dropped a file folder on her desk. It rested on top of a tower of papers. "How was the funeral?"

"Just fine," she answered. She didn't feel like sharing the events of the past few days with anyone yet. It was too much.

"Nice to be back," she said, returning the smile. It felt like she had never left. The desk was familiar, a little awkward. She fired up her computer, logged in, and began to read the events of the past four days. She rubbed her eyes, trying to focus on the screen. It didn't take long before the rhythm returned, but staying up all night was going to be tough. She would have to rely on strong, hot coffee.

At two a.m., she met in the conference room with the other detective working on the Alderman's son's homicide, Mario Perales. He was always prompt.

"Hey, Flynn," he said, with a big smile. "I'm so happy to see you back at work."

"Me, too." Ella was already seated, sipping her coffee, and reviewing her notes. "Anything interesting happen while I was away?" The file on the table was marked "Elijah Thomas."

Perales sat down across from her. He didn't waste any time. "The Alderman is fast-becoming a vocal critic of the Chicago Police Department. He wants somebody's ass in jail, and he wants it right now."

She glanced up at him. "Have we interviewed the usual suspects?"

He nodded. "It might turn out to be a drive-by with an unintended victim."

"Was he in a gang?" It was hard not to be affiliated with a gang in Chicago. "How old was he again?" She thought he was nineteen.

"Nineteen. He might have had a superficial alliance." Perales's eyes started to close, and he shook his head. "This is the longest night," he said.

"That's a fact," she said. The discussion dragged on until an informal plan was written and Perales returned to his side of the office. She opened the file at her desk to reacquaint herself with the facts of the case. Progress needed to be made on it.

After an hour of deliberation, Ella opened a window and sat on the inside ledge, listening to the night sounds of the city from the third floor of the building. It was something she had done so many times before. It was a cacophony of police car sirens, ambulance sirens, screeching tires, and the guttural grinding noises of trucks wheezing and groaning as they changed gears. Automobile horns provided sort of a subliminal staccato background to the constant racket. It never changed. She had grown up with the noise of trains and buses on a twenty-four-hour loop. She used to find it soothing in an odd way, but tonight it was uncomfortable and unwelcome. The exhaust from the cars and trucks seeped in through the window. She closed it, and coughed.

The office was quiet. Several detectives had been called out to an active crime scene, leaving Ella and Perales on their own. When it finally reached the end of her shift, she headed home to her mother's house.

It really wasn't her mother's house anymore, since her mother was no longer there, but Ella referred to it as her mother's house. It was built in 1890 on West Byron Street in Wrigleyville. Her mother bought it after Ella left home, so they could have easy access to Cubs games. It was small, cluttered, and homely. She was comfortable in it, but it still didn't feel like it was hers.

She pulled into the garage off the alley, and went it. The sun was up. She hated the winter when it was still dark out when she got home after a night shift. The days were getting shorter and autumn showed its colors in the red ferns.

In the hallway, she unbuckled her belt and dropped it, listening for the clunk as her gun hit the floor behind her. Keys and phone were tossed on the counter. By the time she reached the bathroom, her clothes were strewn across the floor and she was naked. She stood in the shower for a long time, crying. She missed Jackson Lee.

She heard her phone ring as she toweled herself off, and grabbed it hoping it was him. But it was Brad and she wasn't ready to talk with him. She put the phone down and turned it off, went to bed. As tired as she was, she found sleep elusive. It was always hard to sleep during the day, even with the drapes pulled and the light blocked. Today it was worse, because her thoughts kept returning to Prosper and what she left behind there.

Finally, Ella dozed off. She didn't hear her phone ring again, so Jackson Lee's call went to voice mail.

Chapter 29
Mary Ellen's Mother
Saturday morning

Chief Lovey Jones

Finding Lucille Bellacourt's little house hadn't been all that easy, but Chief Lovey Jones wasn't the type of guy to give up. It turned out she lived close to the Altamaha River in a small house that had been flooded so often, mildew inched up to the window bottoms and the saggy wooden porch bowed in the middle. The land was boggy in the spring and fall, but today it was solid red clay.

A gang of gnats attacked the Chief when he opened his car door, and followed him up the two stairs to the springy porch, buzzing around his head. The wood creaked and threatened to split under his weight.

His knock was answered by a woman of indeterminate age, somewhere between thirty and sixty. She had long, gray hair but her face was smooth and almost devoid of wrinkles. She also had milky blue eyes and the beginnings of a mustache any young man would have been proud of. She wore a pale cotton dress, washed until the material was transparent in places.

"Yeah?" she asked, through the screen door.

"Good afternoon, ma'am," the Chief said, with a big, friendly smile. "I'm Chief Lovey Jones from Prosper. I called you earlier this morning." Although he was wearing his uniform and hat, he showed her his badge. "Are you Lucille Bellacourt? Mother of Mary Ellen Bellacourt?"

"Yeah, that's me. Come on in."

A musty, fetid smell wafted out of the house when the screen door opened. He tried not to breathe. "Why, thank you ma'am." He removed his hat, holding it in his hand. "I wanted to tell you how sorry we are about the loss of your daughter, and possibly take a little bit of your time to ask a few questions." He smiled a sympathetic smile. "I'm sure this is very difficult for you."

"I don't get visitors much," she said. An obvious apology for the lack of cleanliness inside. The house appeared to be the ultimate cat sanctuary and litter box and no doubt was the source of the smell. Newspapers and magazines cascaded in piles in front of, and alongside the cat-covered sofa. A gray cat was asleep on top of the stove, and the Chief almost stepped on a long-haired white cat as it skittered past his legs. It left puffs of feathery fluff on his dark pants.

"I like cats," he lied.

"You can sit there," she said, pointing to a chair next to the sofa.

He looked at the chair and the cat that occupied it, and the cat hair that covered it. "I'll stand, if you don't mind." He smiled. "I've got back trouble. Doctor told me to stand up more."

"Suit yourself," she said, picking up an orange tabby and taking his place on the sofa. He meowed loudly when she tossed him on the floor. "What do you want to know?"

He leaned against the kitchen wall and took out a notebook and pen, asking himself how long a person could live without actually breathing through their nose. He placed his hat on the cleanest part of the counter and hoped for the best. "I'm pretty sure we've got the basic information on your daughter, Mary Ellen." He glanced at Lucille. "She is your daughter, is that right?"

She nodded. "Yes, sir, she is."

"Any brothers or sisters?"

"Nope. She's an only."

"Father?"

"Nope." He didn't pursue that answer.

"When was the last time you saw Mary Ellen?" He watched her intently.

"I suppose it was Sunday, last week."

"Can you say for sure it was Sunday?" He didn't like shifty responses, and words like suppose, maybe, could have been.

"Yes. Sunday."

"What did she do that day? Please be as detailed as you can be." He was scratching notes out as fast as he could.

Lucille gazed at the cat on the stove like it had the answer. "All right. She got up late morning, about eleven, and got dressed."

He interrupted her. "Can you describe what she was wearing?"

"Lemme think about it. It was a pink halter top, and a pair of shorts. They were white shorts. And flip-flops."

It was consistent with the autopsy report. "Then what'd she do?"

"That Junior boy came over and picked her up. She never tells me where she's going. I'm just her mother." Lucille shook her head. The Chief was aware that people commonly spoke in the present tense about those who had passed away. He disregarded it.

"What time was that?"

"Noon. Around noon. Then he dropped her off about two-thirty, and left. She was a little crabby."

"Why's that?" he asked.

"Dunno. Mary Ellen was a moody bitch. Everybody said so." Common knowledge.

The Chief smiled and chuckled to himself. "What happened next?"

"She got a phone call and went into the bathroom to talk, because she didn't want me to hear what she was saying. When she came out, she said she needed to use my car." Lucille looked at Chief Jones. "She didn't have a driver's license, but she's been driving for years," she explained.

"I see," he said. "What time was that?"

Lucille checked the ceiling to see if the answer was written there. "She got home at two-thirty, so it was probably three o'clock when she left." Lucille frowned. "I haven't seen my car since."

"Can you describe the car for me?" The Chief made a note. "I'm going to need your car's license and registration. Do you have that?"

"I can find it, I think. It was blue. Dark blue Chevy, with four doors. About ten years old. Probably more. My brother gave it to me."

"We'll see if we can find it for you." He read over his notes. "If I wrote this down right, the last time you saw Mary Ellen, and your car, was three o'clock, Sunday afternoon."

"Yes, sir."

"I don't suppose you know where she went, do you?" It was unlikely.

"Nah. She never tells me nothin'. I'm just her mother. Let me show you some pictures while you're here." She walked over to a table and sorted through a small pile of photos. The Chief joined her.

The pictures were of a young girl, very thin and pale. She was outside in the nook of a tree limb, sitting on a rock by the river. The photos aged her from a toddler to a teenager, but her unsmiling face never changed.

"That's my Mary Ellen," she said, with a faint smile. "She was a good girl." She grabbed a tissue and dabbed at her eyes.

Lucille sat down back down on the sofa, this time she picked up a sleeping cat to occupy her lap. It never woke up. "What else do you want to ask me?"

The Chief hesitated. "I guess there's no good way to say this. Did you know Mary Ellen was pregnant at the time of her death?" It was an awful question.

"She didn't tell me, but the Coroner did." Tears streamed down her cheeks. When she stopped crying, and took a deep breath, Lucille blew her nose. He leaned back against the kitchen wall, and waited patiently for an opening.

"Besides Junior Wheeler, did she go out with anyone else?"

"Not really. Some man called her a few times. Wouldn't tell me his name, though. Just said to have her call him."

The Chief was interested. "Did he leave a phone number?" He surreptitiously held his nose closed to block the smell from the kitchen where a litter box was placed.

"If he did, I threw it away," she said. "It's not my job to keep track of her boyfriends." Then she remembered her daughter was dead, and the tears began again.

He waited, then changed the subject. He asked what type of activities Mary Ellen participated in.

Her mother was thoughtful. "High school wasn't a lot of fun for her, so she stopped going. She never quite fit in. Didn't play sports. Didn't have any friends. She did hang out a lot at the Catholic Church in Prosper. The one with the roof that isn't flat. Father Santos. He's a wonderful man. So caring. He took a personal interest in Mary Ellen." She smiled as she remembered.

"She went there a lot?"

"Every week," Lucille said. "Oh, I almost forgot." Her eyes lit up. "Mary Ellen was talking to a big model agency in New York."

"About what?" he asked, interested.

"About going to New York to be a model, what else?" Lucille smiled. "She sent them some pictures." In a hushed voice, she added:

"They were naked pictures, but Mary Ellen told me they weren't smutty because they were art." She smiled. "They told her to send one-thousand-dollars to their bank account, and they would get her a bus ticket to New York, and a contract with a big agency. They would even find her an apartment."

The Chief groaned inside. Undoubtedly Internet scam artists sucking money out of the pockets of innocent people. "She was pretty excited about this?"

"She sure was." Lucille frowned. "Now she won't ever get her big break."

"I guess not. That's too bad. Did she have that much money to send?"

Lucille's eyes were wide open. "Of course not."

"Do you know how she planned to come up with that much money?" The Chief thought this was an integral part of the case.

"She told me she had it all worked out, and she was so excited."

"When did she tell you that?"

"I guess it was Sunday. Before she left with Junior."

"Lucille, could I take a look at Mary Ellen's bedroom?" He was beginning to fill in the blanks about her life.

The small room's curtains were closed against the sunlight, making it dark and dusty. The mattress rested on the floor with a thin blanket pulled partially over it. No sheet. One pillow. There were a few small piles of clothes. Several pictures of young pop stars were taped to the walls, along with a big poster of Times Square in New York.

The biggest surprise to Chief Jones was on top of her dresser. Expensive cosmetics covered the entire surface. Lipsticks, eye colors, eye liners, hair pieces, and more, with a lighted oval mirror on a stand.

"Did Mary Ellen have a job?"

"Of course not. She didn't have a car or anything." She rolled her eyes.

"These things are pricey," he said, pointing to the makeup on the dresser. "How did she pay for them?"

"Beats me. She always seemed to have some money on her. A friend would pick her up and they'd go out at night. She'd come home with a few bucks. She told me she was babysitting."

Chief Jones thought it was better that she remain naïve about her daughter's activities. If he had to guess, he figured she was making money the old-fashioned way. Prostitution.

She had very few clothes in her closet. An empty suitcase was open on the floor. She definitely looked like she was ready to leave. "Thanks for letting me see her room." They walked back to the front room.

The Chief closed his notebook and put away his pen. He picked his hat up off the greasy counter, and winced. He'd have to have it cleaned. "Thank you very much, ma'am, for talking with me in such a terrible time. Did Mary Ellen have a computer?"

"No, we don't have a computer. What a silly question."

"I don't suppose her phone is here?" He smiled.

"If she's not here, her phone's not here." It seemed Lucille had run out of patience.

Is it all right if I call you if I have a question or two?"

"Sure." She nodded her head.

"And if you think of anything else, will you call me?" He handed her a card with his phone numbers on it.

"Yes, sir," she said, smiling now. "I want you to find out who killed my little girl, just like you do."

"That's what I intend to do," he said, opening the screen door and stepping out on the porch. He took a deep breath of fresh air, and swatted the gnats out of his way to the patrol car. He needed to take a shower.

He hated cats.

Chapter 30
Ella
Saturday afternoon

Chicago

Ella woke up so groggy, she wasn't sure where she was. It was very quiet. There was no Walter whining to go out or eat breakfast. There was no clicking of doggy nails on the hard floor. And, for the first time in memory, he hadn't locked himself in the bathroom. She missed him. She put on a t-shirt and shorts.

She was very happy to see her coffee maker. She filled it with cold water, popped in a coffee pod, and less than a minute later, she had a steaming cup of coffee. With the cup in hand, she grabbed her phone and sat down in a chair.

She listened to Jackson Lee's voice mail, and smiled. She called him back.

"I'm glad you arrived safely." His voice was mellow, soothing.

"I made it. I worked all night, and I was sleeping when you called. I'm sorry," she said.

"It's wonderful to talk with you," he said. "I'm in the middle of something with a family right now, so I need to be brief."

"Just hearing your voice is enough for me."

"I'll call later, if that's all right."

"Of course, she said." The call was far too short. Hearing his voice was really not enough. Not today.

Her phone rang again, and she answered thinking it was Jackson Lee calling back. It was Brad.

"Hey, you're back, Flynn. Why didn't you call me?"

He always called her by her last name like they did at work. It was so irritating. "The name is Ella," she said.

"Crabby Ella. Did you have trouble sleeping?" He was always cheerful.

"As a matter of fact, I did," she said.

"Do you want me to pick you up some supper on my way over tonight?" Ella had to nip this in the bud. She wasn't ready to see him yet.

"Not tonight. I've got jet lag," she said.

"Jet lag from Atlanta? Isn't that like a two- or three-hour flight?"

She stuck with her story. "I'm very sensitive to time changes."

He sounded disappointed. "Okay, then tomorrow."

"Yes. Tomorrow." They ended the call.

She wasn't looking forward to it at all. She searched the kitchen for something reasonably edible. The bread was moldy and couldn't be salvaged. A trip to the grocery store tomorrow after work would be a good idea. Tonight, having a pizza delivered was the only alternative. Chicago deep-dish pizza. Jackson Lee would love it.

There he was again, in her thoughts. She could close her eyes and know the shape of his face, the scent of his aftershave, the touch of his hand on her cheek. Her career in Chicago had seemed so important, along with her omnipresent fear of the unknown. Now that she was back, she felt so alone. She hoped she'd feel more comfortable as the days passed.

She ate the pizza, then dressed for work, tightening the thick leather belt around her hips. The gun had been checked and rechecked before she put it in the holster. She wound her long, dark hair into a tight bun at the base of her head so it would stay out of the way, especially if she was called to a crime scene. She faced her reflection in the mirror. White button-down blouse, black slacks, jacket to cover up her gun. Back to work. She didn't seem to have the energy she had before. One more thing that time would take care of. Time, and a few more hours of sleep.

Chapter 31
Mayor Wheeler
Saturday

Mayor Big Dick Wheeler

His office was his port of refuge these days. Maud couldn't seem to stop crying and Princess wouldn't come out of her room. Junior sat on the sofa and ate food like his ship was going down, watching movies and wasting time. A second interview with the Chief was scheduled for tomorrow and so far, he didn't think it had gone too well.

Junior came home frazzled from his first interview. He had his phone back, but Chief Jones kept his gun. Big Dick figured he would, so no surprise there. Everything so far was circumstantial evidence. The problem was when you tied it all together, Junior fit the role of the girl's killer. The only thing they didn't have was a video of him pulling the trigger.

He sat at his desk and dropped a few antacids in his palm from the bottle that was always at hand. He felt miserable. Not just his health, but he was sure he made the wrong decision about Mary Ellen. They should have paid her off, then she would have gone away.

He sighed. Who was he kidding? She was a succubus, plain and simple. Destroying his son with her sexual powers. She might have gone away, but she would have come back. And what if she had that baby? Junior would have been tethered to her for the rest of his life. They all would have been.

He loosened his belt and took two more antacids. They'd probably know tomorrow which way the wind was blowing for Junior. He didn't blame the Chief. He blamed the succubus.

Chapter 32
Brad
Sunday late afternoon

Chicago

Ella had somehow missed Jackson Lee's call back Saturday night, so she texted him. Not quite the same as talking with him. Not even close.

At work Saturday night, she was painstakingly going through Elijah's case file. He seemed like a nice young man. Graduated from high school and started college at Northwestern. He had been on his way home from class, to his parents' house in Bridgeview, when he was shot in his car. It was on a Friday night when things really heat up in the inner city of Chicago. Cameras caught a Lincoln Navigator pull alongside his car and open fire. It was all over in an instant.

So far, no luck on finding the car. She was working her way through a list of his friends to find one who might know why Elijah was targeted.

She put the file away when she was called out to an active crime scene around two a.m. Detective McKelvey grabbed her on his way out, and she was quite willing to go. Even on the darkest night, downtown Chicago was brightly lit. They drove to the South Loop and parked behind a trio of Chicago police vehicles with lights flashing. They waited in the background until they understood what had just happened.

There was a female body on the ground framed with yellow crime scene tape. She had been shot in the abdomen, and probably bled out. She was dead. The Evidence Technician was busy collecting trace evidence and taking pictures of the scene. Detective McKelvey was talking to a patrolman.

"We can go back to the station, Flynn. We'll get the report later." She nodded, and got back in the car with him. "What happened?" she asked.

"It was a domestic dispute. They think her husband shot her, and they've taken him downtown for booking." He sighed, and put the car in reverse. "Third shooting tonight in this neighborhood."

"Try not to keep track," she told him. "It only makes it worse." She watched the lights from the squad cars dance all over the brick buildings. It made Prosper seem a universe away from her.

After her shift, she drove home even more tired than she was the night before. She dropped her clothes on the floor and went straight to bed. Constant knocking woke her up. She quickly pulled on her shorts and t-shirt to answer the door.

It was Brad, a big smile on his face, and a big pizza in his hands. "Hey, babe," he said. "I thought you'd be up by now." He strutted in and put the pizza on the counter. Ella had forgotten how blue his eyes were.

"What time is it?" She had been dead to the world.

"It's four o'clock," he said, pointing to his watch.

He grabbed her in a friendly hug. "I missed you. Why didn't you call me while you were gone?"

She honestly never even considered it, but she wouldn't tell him that. "We were so busy. Time just flew by." She glanced at his face, and he seemed fine with her answer. She went into the bathroom to clean up, and picked up her clothes.

When she came out, he had a mischievous grin on his face. "How about if we head to the bedroom and I show you how much I missed you?"

"No," she said, a little too loudly. "I can't today. You know how it is, right?" She couldn't imagine being intimate with him with Jackson Lee on her mind.

He seemed disappointed, but accepted the night without sex. "We should eat the pizza while it's hot anyway." They both sat down on the sofa and turned on the TV. He took the remote and turned on the news.

The pizza wasn't hot. It wasn't even warm, but it was edible. When they finished eating, Brad leaned over and kissed her. "Did you miss me?"

Had he always kissed her like that? It was too long, and too wet. Ella did not like it at all. She was very uncomfortable and took the pizza box into the kitchen. She didn't answer him.

She watched him spread out on the sofa with his head on the arm, searching through the channels and scrolling on his phone. He hadn't asked her a single question about her trip to Georgia, or her deceased father. As a matter of fact, they never talked at all. She had been thinking about it since before she went to Prosper, and decided that today was the day.

She sat down in the middle of sofa, forcing him to sit up, and took the remote away from him. She turned off the TV. "Listen Brad, I need to talk with you."

He appeared puzzled. "Did I do something wrong?"

She smiled and held his hand. "No. Not at all. It's not going to feel like it at first, but I'm going to do you a big favor."

He put his arm around her and waited for her to continue. She remembered how she had loved the way he held her, how they had enjoyed each other. It seemed like it was long ago. She studied his face.

"I'm going to let you go," she said. "It's not your fault. It's mine. I've changed."

"Why? I love you, Ella." He seemed like he might cry.

"You are the sweetest, nicest guy I know, and you need to find the right woman to love you. It's not me. I'm so sorry." She patted him on the back.

His response quickly changed to anger. "Is there another guy?"

"No," she said. She had decided to break up with him long before she met Jackson Lee. He was not the catalyst. Her phone rang but she didn't answer it.

He stood up and grabbed his keys. When he turned to look at her, she could see the fire in his eyes. "This isn't over," he said. "Nobody walks out on me."

This was a side of Brad she hadn't seen before, and it scared her. He was a big guy, worked out a lot, and boxed in his spare time. She walked over to him, trying to calm him down.

"Please don't be angry, Brad. We can still talk about it, okay?"

He didn't answer. Turned and walked out the door.

She hoped he could find a way to calm down without drinking. He was a nasty drunk, and if he started out pissed off, it would only get worse. By tomorrow, everybody at the police station would know what happened. She would be blamed for breaking Brad's heart, no matter whose fault it was. Her popularity, tenuous as it was, was going to nosedive so she might as well expect it.

It was stupid to date someone she worked with. She knew it and did it anyway. *I'm an idiot*, she thought, picking up her phone to see who called. It was Jackson Lee, and he didn't leave a message.

Chapter 33
Interview #2 Junior Wheeler
Sunday

Chief Lovey Jones

Junior Wheeler was timid this time when he walked in the door and waited for Chief Jones to ask him into his office.

The Chief waved him in and pointed to the seat in front of his desk. "Thanks for coming, Junior. I had a few more questions to ask you." He hit the record button. "You know I'm recording this, right?"

"Yes, sir," he said, sitting down, taking off his cap.

"I spoke with Mary Ellen's mother and she corroborated your story that you dropped the girl off at home around two-thirty Sunday afternoon."

Junior nodded his head, and smiled.

The Chief paused. "Did you know she wanted to go to New York to be a model?"

"Yes, sir. It's all she talked about."

"Mary Ellen had big plans. I see that. That was a lot of money, though. What did you think of that?"

He fidgeted in his chair and brushed the hair back from his face. "They said they'd give her a modeling contract."

"How much money did she need? I don't remember." The wrinkles creased on his forehead.

Junior fidgeted. He wished his father was there to tell him what to say, or not say. "I think she said it was a thousand dollars, maybe."

"Were you going to give her some money to help her out? She was your girlfriend, after all. That would be the thing to do. Did she ask you for money?"

He nodded. "Yeah, she wanted me to help her out, but my dad didn't want to give her any money."

"Why not?" The Chief acted surprised.

Junior shrugged his shoulders. "He didn't like her."

"She seems like a lovely young woman to me. Why wouldn't he want to help her out?"

"It's just that he thought…" His voice trailed off.

"I didn't catch that, Junior. What did you say?"

"He thought she was setting me up." His face was pale and he squeezed his hands into fists.

"Setting you up for what?" The Chief wanted to hear him say it.

"You know, setting me up to make me give her money."

The Chief waited. "I guess I just don't understand. Why would you have to give her money?

"Because of the baby." As soon as he said it, Junior knew he'd made a grave mistake.

"That's right," the Chief agreed. "She was pregnant, wasn't she?"

Junior shut his eyes. "Yes, sir."

"So Big Dick thought she'd use her pregnancy to extort money from you. Is that what I heard you say?"

"She did. She told me she wanted money for an abortion and a thousand dollars to go to New York."

"When did she tell you this, Junior? It sounds like she was drawing a line in the sand."

"Sunday," he said, quietly.

The Chief sat back in his chair and crossed his legs. "Let me get this straight. On Sunday, when you dropped her off at home around two-thirty, you knew that she was pregnant, and she wanted money from you to take care of it, and go to New York. Am I right?"

"Yes, sir." He was aware of how badly the interview had gone for him. His father would be furious.

The Chief needed to know if he had an alibi for Sunday afternoon. "After you dropped Mary Ellen off at her house, where did you go?

Junior shrugged his shoulders. "I went home."

"What time did you get home?"

"I dunno. Probably three o'clock."

"Was there anybody else home who saw you there?"

"No."

"What did you do?"

"Watched TV. Ate a sandwich."

"You were alone all afternoon. Is that right?"

"Yes, sir."

"What time did someone else come home?"

"I fell asleep on the sofa. My mom got home around seven o'clock."

"Let me review this, Junior. You were home from three o'clock to seven o'clock Sunday afternoon, alone. Did anyone call you, or come over, or see you at home?"

"No, sir. I fell asleep on the sofa."

"You have no alibi for Sunday afternoon when Mary Ellen was killed."

His eyes got really wide. "No, I don't." He wished he had thought of something before he was asked the question. He could have lied about it.

"I think we'll call it a day, Junior, at least for now. Stay around town, though, and I'll be in touch." He watched Junior leave as quickly as he could.

The Chief smiled, but he wasn't at all happy with the outcome. Junior had given him more than enough information for him to have an arrest warrant issued. He would have preferred to believe he wasn't guilty.

The Chief planned to talk it over with the Wayne County Judge, but it looked pretty cut and dry from here. He walked out of his office. Bobby Dean was sitting at one of the desks, probably eavesdropping. Connie had left for the day. He wondered what he was going to make for supper tonight.

Chapter 34
Ella
Monday morning

Chicago

Ella came home from work and dropped everything on the floor, including her phone and her keys. She hated her job and she didn't know why. A week ago, she loved being a Chicago cop. She had a great boyfriend. They went to baseball games and drank at the bar with the other cops. Her life was amazing.

Now she wanted to stand in the middle of the room and scream. But she didn't, because her neighbors would call the police. She picked her phone up from the floor. Another missed call from Jackson Lee. And a call from a Georgia area code that left a voice mail message. It was Jake.

"Yeah, hi, Detective. This is Jake from the bar. You told me to call you if I had any information about your dad's death. I didn't find Larry, but I got an address for his mom. She still lives close to Prosper. So, if you want it, give me a call. Bye."

"This is it," she shouted out loud. "This is what I need!" She danced around in a circle, and sat down to call Connie.

She answered on the first ring, as usual. "Connie," Ella said. "What's shakin?"

"Just my ass," she said, and laughed. "What's going on with you, girl?"

"I might just have to come back to Prosper to follow up on a new lead." She was happy for the first time in days.

"I don't know on what, because everything seems to be over and done with."

"What do you mean?"

"The Chief is getting an arrest warrant for Junior Wheeler for the murder of Mary Ellen, otherwise known as the body in the river." She knew Ella would be surprised.

"Really? Wow." She never thought Junior did it. She had always thought the crime was connected to her father's death. That was why she needed to talk to Larry-with-the-Limp. This was so wrong.

"Listen, Connie, I need to ask you about Jackson Lee. I keep missing his calls. Have you seen him lately?"

She was suddenly very quiet. "I saw him yesterday when I was eating at the café. He walked past with a woman I've seen visit him before. They were holding hands."

Ella felt like she'd been sucker-punched. "Oh," was all she could say. Her greatest fear was that she had waited too long. He had run out of patience. She couldn't talk anymore.

"Listen, I'll call you later, Connie." She had to sit down for a while.

She called Chief Warner and asked if he had time for her today. Grudgingly, he told her to stop by his office around five o'clock. She lay down in bed, but she couldn't sleep. Memories of Jackson Lee kept her awake. She called him back, but he was with a family, according to his message. She desperately needed his reassurance that he still loved her, still wanted her as much as she wanted him.

When her alarm went off, she took a shower and dressed for work, even though it was early for her shift. She stood outside Chief

Warner's office until he noticed her and told her to come in.

"Okay, Flynn," he said, glancing at her over the top of his glasses. "Let's make this brief, all right?"

"Yes, sir," she said. He was a little extra-rude today. "I know I just got back from Georgia, but I need to go back. Just for a couple of days." She gave him a half-smile.

"You've got a lot of nerve, Flynn." He seemed angry; his face was red. "You were a day late coming back from bereaved, and now you're asking for more time off?"

She knew she'd have to fortify her case for taking time off. "I've been here eight years, Chief, and never asked for time off before."

He glared at her. "Denied."

She did not expect that. "No days off, is that what you're telling me, Chief? Maybe just one day?" She was very angry. She turned around and closed the door. This might get loud.

"I don't think you understand how important this request is to me, sir." She stared directly at him, and didn't blink. "There is only one person who can identify my father's killer, and I have just gotten a lead that tells me how to find him."

The Chief sat back, unimpressed. "Denied," he said again. "All leaves are cancelled. No exceptions." He smiled. It seemed like he was enjoying his power trip.

"Sir," she said. "You are forcing me to choose between solving my father's murder, and being a Chicago cop." She hoped he would understand when he saw it from that angle.

"Denied. Your shift starts at eleven. Be on time. Now, get out of my office, Flynn. Request denied." He waved her off like she was a fly on a picnic plate. He picked up his phone.

She turned around and walked out of his office. Closed the door behind her. She considered her options, then headed down the hallway to the locker room. She opened her locker and carefully stacked the extra clothes and uniforms on the floor, until it was empty. Then she removed her Chicago Police Department Star from her wallet, and left it on the top shelf. She slammed the locker shut and awkwardly picked everything up to carry out to her car. The hallway was quiet and nobody saw her leave. She tossed the clothes into the back seat, and drove home.

At her mother's house, she unplugged all the appliances and turned off the water. She changed into her favorite jeans and Cubs t-shirt, hi-tops, and added her Cubs hat. She threw the clothes she liked into a suitcase along with her leather belt, holsters, and gun. She had to sit on it to close it.

With her trunk full, she pulled out of the alley, then stopped. She typed a brief resignation letter, effective immediately, and sent it to Chief Warner, the HR department, and anyone else she thought might like to know. Her relief was so great, she laughed and cried at the same time. It was wonderful to be free. All these years she thought police chiefs were supposed to be like Chief Warner, until she met Chief Lovey Jones. It turns out Chief Warner was just an asshole. She laughed again, put her car in drive, and headed south to Georgia.

When she crossed the state line, the sky filled up with grey clouds. To the south she saw a black line of thundershowers. The closer she came to Prosper, the darker the clouds were until they burst with rain that pelted her car.

Chapter 35
Ella's Back
Tuesday Noon

Ella tried to drive straight through, but ended up stopping halfway to sleep a couple of hours in her car. It made the fifteen-hour trip longer, but she arrived safely, which she decided was a good idea. It was still very dark and rainy when she drove through town. The storm followed her.

Her first stop was the Armstrong Funeral Home. She was desperate to see Jackson Lee. Her knock was answered by Martha, who gave her a hug, and invited her in. When he saw her, his face broke out in a big smile. He picked her up off the floor and swung her around like she weighed nothing at all. It ended in a hug, and that ended in a kiss. "Connie told me you were on your way. I've been waiting for you."

"It's so good to see you." She smiled. "I've missed you so much."

"How many days do you have this time?"

"As many days as I want," she said, smiling. "I quit my job."

He laughed. "That is music to my ears." From the direction of the kitchen, they heard the clacking of big toenails on the floor hustling toward them.

"Walter!" she said. He was howling his "where have you been" yowl, over and over, disappointed and happy all at the same time, wagging his tail.

She knelt and petted his head, squishing his long ears together. He stopped howling. If he could have purred like a cat, he would have.

He licked her hand.

Ella stood back up and kissed him again. "It's so good to see you and talk with you," she said, leaning against him. "I didn't know how much I would miss you until I went back to Chicago."

"Did you drive all night?" he asked, concerned.

"I did, and I'm exhausted. I'm going to stop by and talk with the Chief for just a few minutes, then go home and get some sleep. I'll take Walter with me, if you don't mind?" She glanced up at him.

"I think Walter likes you more than he likes me, so that's just fine." He grabbed a leash hanging by the door, and clipped it on his harness. "Okay if I stop by to see you tonight?"

She smiled and nodded her head. "Is there any doubt?"

"Great," he said. "Call me when you wake up."

"I'll do that." He seemed reluctant to let her hand go. "I'm so glad you came back."

"So am I," she agreed. Everything felt so perfect. She opened the door against the rain. The wind had picked up. It looked like there was another storm on the way.

Chapter 36
The Chief
Tuesday

Chief Lovey Jones was in his office when Ella strolled in with Walter. He stood up right away and gave her a bear hug. "I'm glad to see you, Flynn. Connie told me you were on the way back."

"Thanks, Chief. I'm glad to be back. I actually missed this little town." She smiled at him. What a difference between Chief Warner and Chief Lovey Jones. Walter returned to his little haven under the Chief's desk.

"How many days did you get off?"

"It's a pretty long story, so for now, I'll just say I can stay as long as I want." He seemed puzzled, but he didn't ask any more questions.

She sat down in the chair in front of his desk. "Connie told me you were going to arrest Junior Wheeler for Mary Ellen's death. Is that true?"

"It sure is."

"Before you do, there are a few things I think you should know." He sat back in his chair and waited for her to continue.

"I'm listening."

"Last week Wednesday, the day of the autopsy, when we found out my father was murdered, I went to Jake's Bar to interview him." The chief nodded. "He told me my father had come into the bar scared and shaking, and drank three shots in rapid succession, just to calm down."

She paused. "He didn't ordinarily do that, according to Jake. When his friend, Larry, came in, he told him all about what happened. Then Larry left."

"Jake saw this?"

"Yes, sir, he did. Then my father proceeded to get so drunk that he passed out on the bar, and Jake woke him up at two a.m., closing time." She could tell Chief Jones was wondering where all this was going. "He told Jake that he saw something that terrified him. He said: 'You wouldn't believe what I saw' and that he was afraid to tell anyone. Then he left the bar at two a.m., walked home, and someone killed him inside his house."

"Why didn't you tell me this before?"

"When I finished with Jake," she explained, "I was called back here because you and Bobby Dean had arrested the burglar for not only residential burglary, but also for the murder of my father." She waited for him to process the information.

"Uh huh. Interesting. What is your take on this, Flynn?"

She was chewing on her bottom lip. "I have a theory that my father was down by the river earlier that day, and happened on one, or maybe two, people dumping a body in the river. Sunday afternoon turns out to be the time the GBI established for when Mary Ellen's body went into the river."

"But you don't know that's what he saw."

"No, I don't know for sure. I also believe that he knew the people at the river, which is the part that scared him, and, as it turned out, they knew him, too. When he came home from the bar, they killed him to shut him up."

The Chief considered the situation seriously. "Your theory would indicate that your father could not have been killed by the burglar we arrested."

She nodded in agreement. "I believe it could also mean that Mary Ellen was killed by someone other than Junior Wheeler." She waited for his response, which was slow in coming.

"Maybe. But it could have been Junior Wheeler dumping the body in the river, couldn't it?"

"Yes, sir. Although I don't think knowing it was Junior Wheeler would have frightened my father so badly." Ella had been thinking about it constantly. "I know there is no way I can tie someone else to both crimes without talking to the guy in the bar with my father, Larry-with-the-limp."

"You're right about that, Flynn. This is just an interesting theory right now. You haven't been able to find him?"

"No, sir," she said, shaking her head. "I just haven't had the time to look for him. But Jake has just given me the address for Larry's mother, who still lives close to town, and I believe with her help, I can locate Larry and get the information I need."

"What do you need from me?" he asked.

"Can you hold off on arresting Junior until I find Larry tomorrow? If it turns out to be Junior, you'll just have more good evidence. But if it turns out to be someone else, it might save Junior's life."

"I will do that, Flynn. I don't want to put this boy in jail if he's innocent, and one more day isn't going to make any difference right now."

She was relieved. "Thank you so much for listening to me. I just need one more day. Then we can put this all to rest." She stood up to leave. "I won't take up anymore of your time, Chief."

He stood up, too. "There's just one thing I'd like you to keep in mind, Flynn. If your theory is right, this killer, or killers, have already murdered two people. They won't even flinch if you get in their way. They'll kill you, too."

Scary thought, but she had also considered that. "Thanks, Chief. I will keep that in mind." She smiled. "Hopefully, this will be over tomorrow. Right now, I'm going to go home and get some sleep. I drove all night to get here."

"You do that," he said. "Watch your back."

"I will," she said, waking Walter up. They walked out of his office, practically bumping into Bobby Dean who was leaving in a hurry. He was out the door before they left.

It had stopped raining temporarily. Another thunderstorm was approaching from the north, and it could be even worse than the last one. She planned to sleep through it. Ella hoisted Walter up into the car, and drove to the blue house for a well-deserved nap.

Chapter 37
The Fight
Tuesday Afternoon

The house was so quiet, when Ella heard a floor board creak, she was on instant alert. The only thing that made a floor board squeak, was someone walking on it. She reached under her pillow for her Glock and quietly slid out of the bed, closet-side, facing the door. Her heart was beating so hard, she was sure anybody could hear it, and her hands were clammy.

She inched her way along the walls to the door that led to the hallway, listening for Walter. She heard a scratch on the bathroom door and knew he had locked himself in again. That was the best place for him to be right now. The afternoon sky had become absurdly dark, lit up with shards of lightening and consumed with volleys of thunder. The inside of the house was unlit, and dark.

She had talked herself into believing they wouldn't come after her, but she misjudged how afraid they were of what she might find out. Breathing too fast, she stopped and took several deep breaths to feel more stable, more balanced. She wished she had shoes on. Her feet were bare and wouldn't be much help in a fight.

Her hands were holding the gun in front of her, and they were visibly shaking. Her finger was on the gun's trigger. When a lightning bolt lit up the sky outside, it almost tricked her into firing. Another floor board squeaked, and it sounded closer.

It wasn't quiet anymore as the staccato rain began to beat down on the roof.

She reached the doorway and peered into the hallway. It was empty. To her left was the door that led to the second bedroom. She wanted to be the guy who shot first. She pushed the door open with her foot, took a second to peek in.

He grabbed her from behind. Before Ella could react, she was locked in a vicious chokehold, lifted off her feet, her gun knocked from her hands. It hurtled across the floor and hit the wall with a thud. Gasping for air, she instinctively dropped her chin and kicked back as hard as she could. He grunted when she hit his groin, breaking his chokehold. Her throat was on fire, she fought for air. The black figure fell backward but quickly regained his balance. He had the long arms of a basketball player, no way to stay out of his reach.

He's going to kill me, she thought. Any fear she had felt turned into adrenaline-fueled anger. *Not today, fucker. No fucking way.* Everything switched to slow motion. She tried to see his face under the mask, but only saw the darkness of his eyes. They looked hollow.

She tried to increase the distance between the two of them to stay out of his reach, but he grasped the front of her shirt and slammed her body against the wall. The left-side of her head smacked the wall and left an impression, then bounced off. Her neck hurt. Her ears were pulsing with a stabbing pain, she was groggy. She tasted copper tang and knew her nose was bleeding. She shook her head trying to focus, sprinkling the air with little drops of moisture. He gripped her shirt again, and threw her against the wall, even more violently this time. She turned at the last second and let her shoulder take the full impact, leaving her arm numb and her shoulder throbbing. This time she screamed, but she didn't feel the pain.

The sour smell of sweat was pervasive. He circled her, getting closer, ruthless. Her legs were heavy, clumsy. She tried to get back into a rhythm and find some distance from him, but he was too quick. He put his large, vise-like hands around her neck, squeezing the breath out of her. With a sickening realization, she knew the rasping sound she heard was coming from her.

Prying one of his fingers free, she bit down as hard as she could. He shrieked, pulled his hand away. She grabbed his wrist and sank her teeth into the fleshy part by the thumb, hoping to hear a bone break, glad when she saw blood. When he knocked her head away, she blindly reached up and under his mask, leaving four long scratches on his face. Her fingernails came away with blood and DNA.

But the damage she did wasn't near enough. She was exhausted and light-headed.

"I could have killed you right now, but I didn't. Nobody's going to tell me what to do, ever again." He said it loud enough for her to hear over the ringing in her ears.

When he landed a punch on the side of her head, she never saw it coming. Didn't anticipate it at all. It didn't hurt, but she felt the blow like a brick banging down on her head. The world turned black and there were stars, just like in the cartoons. And a deafening silence with a loud roar in her ears. She started blinking and her legs were wobbly. She had the worst headache.

And that was the last thing she remembered.

Chapter 38
After the Fight
Tuesday

Something just happened, Ella thought. In the distance she heard Jackson Lee calling to her. *Was this a dream or reality? Was he really there?*

She tried to move her head, which was on the floor for some reason.

"Thank God," she heard him say. "Can you hear me? Should I call an ambulance?"

"Yes, I can hear you," she said, "and no, don't call an ambulance." Her voice sounded strange to her. She wasn't sure if she could open her eyes, so she kept them closed. With a shudder, she remembered clearly the punch that hit the right side of her head, but nothing after that. She was afraid to touch her face or move her arms.

"What's the stuff on my face? Is it blood?" Her voice sounded muffled to her, and very far away.

She felt Jackson Lee kneeling next to her, carefully brushing her hair off her face. "It's dried blood. You might have a broken nose there."

"Bastard," she said.

She kept her eyes closed. "Could you look at my teeth?"

She felt him carefully lift her lips to look inside her mouth. "Hard to tell since there's a lot of blood in here, but they look good to me."

"Awesome." *Five-thousand-dollars' worth of orthodontia saved.* She moved her tongue around to make sure. "I'm going to open my eyes now."

"Okay," he said. "Your right eye looks a little swollen, so I think you're going to have a black eye."

She squinted up at him. "Things are a little fuzzy, but my eyes work." She moved her legs and arms. "Nothing seems to be broken."

"Do you want me to help you sit up?"

"I do. If I scream, ignore it." He put his hands under her arms from behind, and guided her to a sitting position on the floor. "Oof," she said.

"It looks like your nose is bleeding again."

"Fucking bastard broke my nose."

"Do you know who it was?"

"He was wearing black, even a black ski mask, and everything happened really fast."

Jackson Lee started to wash her face with a warm washcloth. "When you finally stand up, if anything feels broken, except your nose, obviously, I'm taking you to the hospital. Understand?"

She glared at him with squinty eyes. "Okay."

"Now, tell me what happened."

Chapter 39
The Police Report
Tuesday

When Walter came out of the bathroom, he was jet propelled. He howled at Ella, he howled at Jackson Lee, then ran outside. He stood and peed for a very long time.

Chief Jones pulled up a kitchen chair and sat opposite Ella and Jackson Lee on the sofa. She was lying down with her head in his lap. "I feel awful," she said. Her voice was hoarse, her throat bruised and sore.

Officer Connie stood at the entrance to the kitchen, leaning against the door jamb. "I think that's reasonable, honey," she said. "You look like shit."

Ella had a new band-aid across her nose with a splint holding it carefully in place. There was a large lump on the right side of her head, and the skin around her right eye was swollen and tight, already showing a bruise. "I'm watching her for signs of a concussion," Jackson Lee said to no one in particular. No one answered.

Chief Jones opened the notebook on his lap and readied his pen. "Do you know who the intruder was?"

Ella thought about it. "No. He was dressed in black and he was wearing a black ski mask. He was fairly tall. Long arms," she said, remembering his reach. She coughed, then drank from a water bottle. Coughed again. "I did get a sample of his DNA under my fingernails when I scratched his cheek." She smiled. "And he said the strangest thing right before he knocked me out."

"What was that?"

"He said he could have killed me, but he didn't. Nobody tells him what to do anymore."

Jackson Lee smiled. "I'm grateful for that."

"Me, too," the Chief agreed. "I'm glad he decided in your favor. We'll have to get that DNA from you." He called Connie over. "Get an evidence bag and tag it with the DNA." He turned to Ella. "I told you that might happen. What bothers me, though, is how quickly they found out you were back. You've only been here a few hours."

"Yes," she said. "That puzzles me, too." She had only been asleep for about an hour.

"Was your door unlocked?"

"Not the front door, but the back door is usually open. Walter prefers it that way." The dog wagged his tail when he heard his name, then went back to sleep. She coughed again, and her chest hurt. "He probably came in the back door." Ella was angry with herself for being so negligent. You'd never leave a door unlocked in Chicago.

"All right," the Chief said. "You were asleep when he came in. Did he come in the bedroom?"

"No. I heard the floor board squeak. Right at the entrance to the hallway, there's a board that does that every time you step on it."

"Then what did you do?"

I grabbed my Glock from under my pillow, and started looking for him. I made it to the small bedroom when he jumped me from behind, knocking my gun away. He had me in a chokehold, off the ground."

"You broke the chokehold."

"I did, then he started slamming me against the wall." Ella stared into space, remembering the beating she took. "I was really tired. My ears were ringing and lights were flashing. Then, from out of the blue, he punched me in the head." She pointed to the large lump on the right side of her head. "After that, everything turned black. And that's all I can remember." Exhausted by her response to the Chief's question, she lay back down on Jackson Lee's lap. Her voice was fading.

"And then you came in?" The Chief nodded at Jackson Lee.

"I did. I don't know how long she was knocked out, but she was supposed to call me, and when she didn't, I decided to come over." He smiled down at Ella. "What a mess."

"Thank you," she said, smiling back. "I don't know what I would do without you."

"I guess there isn't much more to ask." The Chief stood up and pocketed his notebook and pen. "We'll leave you to get some rest." He looked concerned. "I'm so sorry this happened to you, Flynn," he said. "I wouldn't want it to happen to anyone, but especially not you."

She smiled at him. Her teeth had been brushed and the blood was washed away. "I appreciate that, Chief," she said. "It hasn't been my best day." The last remaining voice she had was starting to squeak.

Connie came over to the sofa, took a DNA sample from under her fingernails on her right hand, and gave her a kiss on the cheek. "It's gonna be a better day tomorrow," she promised. Ella gave her a thumbs up. The Chief left at the same time they heard Connie rev up her bike. Jackson Lee closed the door behind them.

"I'm fixin' to make you some soup, so close your eyes and take a nap," he ordered.

And she did.

Chapter 40
That Night
Tuesday

After Ella ate her soup and drank her sweet tea, she lay back down on the sofa. Jackson Lee found a soft pillow for her, and a clean-smelling blanket from the closet. She was barely awake.

"Will you stay with me tonight?" she asked, sounding a little desperate.

"Of course." He sat down next to her. "I was planning on it." He looked more concerned than he sounded. "Are you sure you're okay?"

"Yes. Thank you. I'm a little worried he'll come back and finish the job."

He brushed her damp hair away from the lump on her head and checked her nose bandage. The shower had washed away the sweat and blood, but not the bruises. "No. He won't be back. Besides, I'd have Walter kill him if he did."

"He might howl at him until he died, but that's about it."

Ella's gaze met Jackson Lee's, and her heart felt like it flipped over. The look in his eyes was so tender, so intimate. "How are you feeling," he asked. "Really."

"My body feels battered and bruised. But what hurts the most is how vulnerable I feel now. It's not a familiar feeling for me. I thought I was the toughest guy in town." She smiled a wan smile. "Reality sucks."

"You're not alone," he said, puffing up her pillow. "I'm here. I'll never hurt you, and I'll never leave you." He smiled. "I'm gonna make you part of my life now that you're back home."

"Thank you. And thank you for finding me, and taking care of me. And feeding me." She did feel overwhelmed with gratitude.

"I love you," he said, and stood up. "Now get some sleep. If you need anything, just call out." She was surprised he said he loved her, but she knew it was true.

"Can you sit here beside me until I fall asleep?"

He smiled. "Absolutely." He sat down beside her again on the sofa.

"Tell me a story."

He pursed his lips in thought. "Once upon a time, a boy met a girl and he loved her more than anyone has ever loved before…" Ella had already fallen asleep. He pulled the blanket up and tucked her in. He kissed her on the cheek. "I love you. Sleep well."

After a while, he went into the bedroom for the night.

Chapter 41
In the Middle of the Night
Tuesday-Wednesday

After falling into a very deep sleep, Ella woke in the middle of the night. It was a struggle to stand up at first, but there was no dizziness. The rotator cuff in her right shoulder might be torn, but her arm still functioned. Walter was blissfully unaware that anything had changed, and she tucked the blanket around him. She felt like everything had changed.

Surviving a life or death experience can cause you to look at your life in a new way. She knew that. Her fight response was instinctual from years of police training, and probably saved her life. But she was having a difficult time moving past the after effects. She didn't care about the bruises. The intruder had violated the sanctity of her home, took away her peace. She was vulnerable. A very uncomfortable feeling.

Slowly, she walked down the hallway, pushed the door open as quietly as she could. Jackson Lee was awake and reading. He watched her from the bed.

"Couldn't sleep," she said.

"Me either. Are you okay?" he asked. "Is your throat still sore? Your voice is raspy."

She sat on the edge of the bed next to him. He was naked except for summer shorts. That excited her. Bronzed by the hot Southern sun, broad shouldered, and well-muscled. He was a handsome man. She had on an extra-large Cubs t-shirt and white shorts.

"I hope you don't mind," she said, smiling, "but I wanted to climb in bed with you." Her voice still sounded far away, and shrill.

He laughed. "Sounds good to me. Which side do you want?"

"Outside. In case I throw up."

"Should I get a bucket?"

"No, I'm just trying to be proactive," she said.

He scooted over in the small bed, making room for her. She climbed in. Ella saw him rub the stubble on his chin. He caught her watching him. "I need a shave," he laughed. "No, you don't," she said. "You're perfect." He wrinkled his nose. "No, I'm not." But she did think he was perfect. She stroked the hair on his chin and the sides of his face.

She fluffed the pillow behind her and sat up.

"Tell me why you left your job," he said, lying on his side, his head propped up by his arm.

"So much has changed in just a couple of days." She looked around the little room. "Jake called me with Larry-with-the-limp's mother's address, and I knew, with this information, I could locate Larry and find my father's killer. When I asked Chief Warner for time off, he said no." She felt the anger rise up in her again. "Even when I told him how important it was to me to find my father's killer, he denied my request."

"Why would he do that?"

"He said all leaves were cancelled. I told him he was forcing me to make a decision between finding my father's killer, and staying a Chicago cop."

"I'm glad you told him that. But he still said no?"

"He did. He told me to be on time for my shift. In other words, he didn't expect me to leave. I think he thought I was making it all up just to get time off."

He waited.

"When I left his office, my mind was made up. I will find my father's killer. I cleaned out my locker, went home and packed a suitcase, emailed my resignation, and left."

"Do you think you made the right decision?" he asked.

She smiled. "One hundred percent. I'm tired of being pushed around. I'd like to be in charge of my life for a change."

He smiled back. "I hope now that you're in charge of your life, you'll include me in it."

She lay down close to him and he put his arms around her. "I'm all in," she whispered. "I love you." He kissed her neck, and her cheek, and her ear.

"Just be with me," he said. "We'll figure out the details later." He smiled at her. "You should know I'm inclined to hold you like this forever."

Ella smiled. His sexy low-country drawl was soothing, and the slow way his words entered the air, spun for a second, and faded away enraptured her. The flavor of his skin, the amber flecks in his eyes, the way his lips parted to reveal his white teeth. She was mesmerized.

"I'd like that," words that barely made any sound. It was really all she could manage. Their heads were close enough to touch. She was having trouble breathing, and it wasn't just because her nose was broken. She brushed his lips with hers. Surprised by the warmth of his mouth, she stopped for a second to say 'careful,' and point to her nose. But that was all the time she could spare. His kisses were irresistible, tantalizing and she couldn't think of anything at all except how she wanted more.

He reached for his phone, and then she heard Barry White singing "I'm gonna love you just a little more, baby." "That's it," she laughed. "You've pushed me over the edge."

Unhurriedly, they sat up. Jackson Lee lifted her shirt over her head and tossed it on the bed. He kissed her eyes, cheeks, and tenderly his lips lingered on her neck. She reached up and pulled the rubber band from her hair, letting her hair flow carelessly down her bare back. His fingers combed through her hair and it was a feeling of pure ecstasy.

When his lips reached her breasts, her breath quickened and she shivered in anticipation. Highlighted by the moon, she stood up and slowly slid her shorts down her legs, revealing all she was. He did the same, then stood next to her, naked.

In the moonlight, she could see everything about him, and he could see everything about her. He placed his hands on the sides of her head and drew her close, bending to kiss her again. This kiss put all the others to shame. She thought her heart had stopped beating. It was passion. She had never truly felt it before.

She lay down on the bed and waited for him.

"I've imagined this since I met you," he whispered. She buried her face between his neck and shoulder and smelled the scent of his skin, tasted the salt, and relished the ardor of his embrace. It felt as though time stopped as they became more familiar with each other's bodies and the way they fit together. In a rush, it was over.

After, they lay close in an embrace. "I love you," Ella said.

"And I love you. I've loved you since I met you last week."

She laughed and kissed his soft lips.

When she woke again, she couldn't remember falling asleep. He lay behind her, and even though he slept, his arms still enveloped her. He was a part of her life now and whatever happened today or tomorrow, he wasn't going anywhere without her.

So, this is what love is.

Chapter 42
A New Day
Wednesday morning

Past dreaming and before the day began, Ella relived each moment of the night before. The new sensations. The incredible passion. Jackson Lee's gentle touch. His arms were still around her. She covered his hands with hers and fell back asleep.

The next time she woke up, she could hear him in the shower. She was still drowsy, swallowing was difficult because her throat was dry and sore. Her neck ached, and her shoulder throbbed. She couldn't breathe out of her nose, but the bandage was intact.

Jackson Lee had a towel wrapped around his hips when he came back in the room. He bent over and kissed her cheek. "Good morning. How are you feeling?"

"Wonderful," she lied. Her voice was still hoarse. She sat up, still naked, and kissed him on the mouth. He dropped the towel. She welcomed him into her arms and they lay back on the bed. This time there wasn't as much urgency and things moved slower. But the passion was equal to the first time. Afterwards, they held each other tight.

This time they showered together and dressed.

"I love you," he said, rubbing her back as they sat on the edge of the bed.

"Me, too. Will you help me tape my nose?" *Such an odd thing to say*, she thought.

"My pleasure," he said. They stood in front of the bathroom mirror while Ella scrutinized her injuries. The bone in her nose was a little skewed where it was fractured, but it didn't look like it would require surgery. Jackson Lee delicately applied a bandage.

Her right eye was swollen and barely open. It was surrounded by an indigo blue background with a touch of dark red for contrast. It was a showstopper. She felt the bump on the side of her head, no longer the size of an egg, it was grape-sized. It was still painful to the touch, and bruising was starting to show.

She tried to raise her right arm. It hurt, but she could do it. Probably not a rotator cuff injury, she hoped. An inventory of random cuts and welts illustrated she was definitely in a very physical fight, and the burgundy-red ring around her neck was a reminder of how close she came to dying.

"I am hideous," she said.

"No, don't be silly. You look fine," he lied. She rolled her eyes at him.

"I'm off to find Larry's mom," she said, foraging through her suitcase for jeans, underwear, and a proper shirt, and dressed quickly. She cinched her thick, leather belt around her hips, slipped the holster onto it, then clipped on a single cloak mag carrier, loaded. She slid her Glock in and spent some time checking the cant and height so she was confident in reaching it quickly and removing it smoothly. Time doing this was never wasted. When she looked up, Jackson Lee was staring at her. Definitely a side of her he had never seen. Her shirt was intentionally big and long to conceal her gun.

"I'll be okay. I'm not going unprepared," she said, reassuringly.

"I have to meet with a family this morning. I wish you'd wait until I can go with you." He looked worried.

"Don't worry. I'll be fine." She kissed him on the cheek.

"Please be careful. He already tried to kill you once."

"Don't remind me," she said with a smile. She was dressed and ready to go. "I refuse to be intimidated."

They stood in the bedroom. Two very different people, on the verge of creating a world that filled them to the top with compassion and love. "I won't be gone long. I promise." He adjusted her Cubs baseball cap and pulled her hair through the hole in back.

I just know I'm going to find him. This is my last chance.

Chapter 43
Finding Larry's mother
Wednesday Morning

According to the address Jake gave Ella, Larry's mother lived not far away from Prosper in a small town named Little Creek. There was an intersection with a stop sign and another sign revealing the population to be 73 souls. A bait shop, liquor store, and closed grocery store sat around the town's center, and several houses lined the street with the possibility of residents.

The crossroad was Magnolia Avenue, and she turned left, as her GPS suggested. She checked behind her to see if anyone was following her. No cars in sight. She drove over a dried-up creek bed under a bridge. *Hence, the name of the town*, she thought. A voice told her she had reached her destination, although she couldn't see a house from the street. She followed a dirt road that led into a grove of trees where a small white house resided.

An older woman with white hair in plaits occupied a rocking chair on the porch, and watched with obvious interest as Ella's car drove up. She smiled and kept rocking.

Ella parked in what might have been a driveway at one time. It was covered with brush now. Her heart was beating quicker, she was excited to talk with the woman, whose expression changed from welcoming to horrified as Ella approached. She had forgotten about her fight injuries.

Ella smiled a big, happy smile. "Sorry. I was in a car accident," she explained. "Don't pay any attention to the nose or the black eye." She saw her relax and smile back. "I'm looking for Ida Pearl Taylor. Am I at the right place?"

"You found her," she said.

"Excellent. Ma'am, do you have a son named Larry?"

"Why, yes, I do."

Ella was relieved, she had to take a deep breath. "I'm really glad to hear that. I'm the daughter of a childhood friend of his, Ray Flynn, and I'm trying to locate Larry. My name is Ella Flynn."

She stopped rocking, and smoothed the lap of her cotton dress. "I know Ray Flynn. He was a wonderful boy. Larry would bring him to our house most evenings for supper." She smiled as she thought back. "I haven't seen him in years, though."

Ella sat on the top step of the porch. "I don't know if you've heard," she began, "Ray, my father, was killed about a week ago. He lived in Prosper."

Ida Pearl put her hand over her mouth, obviously surprised by what she heard. "No, I didn't know that. I'm so sorry, sweetheart. Bless your heart, that's terrible."

Ella nodded in agreement. "Yes, ma'am. It definitely is. It's part of why I'm trying to find your son, Larry. Do you know where he lives?" Her answer would make all the difference.

"I do, but I have to draw you a map. His house isn't easy to find."

Ella radiated happiness. "Wonderful." She pulled out her notebook that she carried in her pocket, along with a pen. "Could you make me a map on this?"

"That's pretty small, but I'll give it a try." She handed the notebook to Ida Pearl, watched her painstakingly create a map with turns and labeled buildings in tiny handwriting. When she handed her notebook back, Ella's heart sank. It looked like a spiderweb, but it was way too late to give up now.

"Thank you, ma'am. I'm so grateful for your help." She gently held her cool, smooth hand. "You are amazing."

She smiled. "Thank you. I love to get visitors. Come back any time."

"I'd love to do that, if I may." She was serious. "I'm going to be in Prosper for a while, and I'll make every effort to stop by again. I'd love to hear more about my father."

"He was a lovely boy," she said. "And a really good eater." Her smiles were endearing, Ella really liked her.

"I can't wait to see you again," she said as she left, "and thank you so much for the map." She walked to her car, then waved goodbye as she reversed down the long, overgrown driveway. Finding Larry-with-the-limp was going to be a challenge, even with a map.

Chapter 44
Finding Larry-with-the-limp
Wednesday

Ella followed every squiggly turn on the map until she was certain she had been down each dirt road that led to the river, and turned down trails that couldn't be classified as dirt roads, even drove over dead lawns and through cemeteries. Where there wasn't a visible path, she stopped the car and walked to see what couldn't be seen from the road.

What houses there were couldn't be classified as houses. They were crudely built shacks with rotting foundations. Definitely a flood zone. The better ones were raised several feet with bricks to escape the spring river water. In some cases, battered old cars littered the yard, weeds growing on their bumpers. Quite a few shacks looked abandoned with no vehicles around.

She was looking for a house with signs of activity, open doors or windows, maybe even one where the weeds were cut. Or smoke from a fire. She had retraced her route for the second time when from a distance, she saw a man in his yard tossing out gray water. He wasn't there earlier. As she watched, he walked back to his house. He was dragging a leg, and had a definite limp. Ella was euphoric.

She quickly turned down a dirt path that led nowhere. She left her car and thrashed her way through stinging nettle and bug-infested brush to reach the shack. She didn't even bother to brush the mosquitos away. Bug bites. *How much worse can I look?* She thought.

The man had already gone inside. Her heart was beating fast as she scaled the three concrete steps to the rotting porch, and knocked loudly on the door.

The man who answered the door was shorter than Ella, almost bald, and dressed in faded jeans and a t-shirt. It was hot and humid outside, it was hot and musty inside. The distinct smell of mildew escaped out the door. She watched his face change from curious to frightened when he saw her black eye and nose splint. She laughed and put her hand on her face. "Sorry. Car accident. I know I look a mess."

"Wow," he said. "You really got messed up."

"It looks much worse than it is," she said, smiling. "My name is Ella Flynn. My father was Ray Flynn. I'm looking for his childhood friend, Larry Taylor. His mother gave me this address."

"I'm Larry," he said. "Yeah, Ray was a friend of mine. Ella. He talked about you a lot." Her heart felt like it flipped over, and she took a deep breath.

She put her hand on her heart, her bottom lip trembled. "That makes me so happy. For years I thought he forgot me."

He smiled. "No, he didn't forget you. Sometimes life gets in the way, that's all. Come on in." He held the door open for her.

She breathed a deep sigh of relief and entered the house. It was small, but uncluttered. It felt cozy to her. He pointed to a chair in the corner. "Sit down and make yourself comfortable. I'll make some sweet tea for us."

Instead of sitting down right away, she looked at the pictures that filled the space on his walls. There were many black-and-white photos that featured people from at least a generation ago, some sepia-stained photographs of long-ago weddings. She smiled at a few pictures of Larry's mother, who hadn't changed all that much through the years. On a short wall, there were more recent color photos.

In particular, Ella inspected a graduation picture. Class of 1985, Jessup High School. The students were dressed in shiny blue gowns with traditional hats, standing in front of the high school. The taller students filled the back row. Larry was in the first row. Very easy to identify. She looked for her father, but she wasn't sure which one he was. She'd have to ask Larry to show her where he was standing.

The clink of ice cubes announced the arrival of the tea. He handed her a glass filled to the top and she gratefully sipped it. "This is wonderful. Thank you." She hadn't anything to drink since this morning, and she was parched.

"Pleasure," he replied, smiling. "Do you like my pictures?"

"Oh, yes. I saw the ones of your mother when she was younger. She's still a beautiful woman, isn't she?"

Larry smiled. "I think so. How did you find her, anyway?"

"Jake from Jake's Bar in Prosper gave me her address so I could locate you."

Ella changed the subject. "I noticed your graduation picture on the wall. Was my father in your class? Could you point him out to me?"

He smiled. "Yes, he was in my class. We went to school together since we were little kids." He pointed to a tall student in the back row with dark hair and a pleasant smile. "That's Ray."

She stood close to the photo and examined every aspect of it to see if she remembered what he looked like. "I see it," she said, excited. "I remember him. Thanks, Larry." She felt like she was given a gift, and it made her happy.

"Ray was my best friend. We did everything together," he said proudly. When he remembered that Ray had died, he frowned. "I'm so sorry he's gone."

"Yes, I am, too," she said. "Would you tell me a little bit about my father? I don't know anything about his childhood." She sat on the chair in the corner.

"Don't mind at all," he assured her. He put his glass down on a table and got comfortable in his chair. "Ray lived in a house by the school. And mine was two streets over."

She tried to imagine it. "Did he have brothers or sisters?"

He shook his head. "No, it was just Ray and his dad. They didn't get along, so he spent a lot of time at my house. Had most of his meals there. My mom tried to help him out because she felt sorry for him."

"She told me he was a good eater," she said, smiling. "I bet your mom was a good cook, wasn't she?"

"She sure was, and she still is. Stop by for Thanksgiving at her house, and you'll see what I mean."

"Be careful what you say. I just might do that."

He chuckled, and continued his story. "By the end of high school, Ray's dad's drinking had gotten so bad, he stayed away as much as he could. He fixed up an old Chevy, and even got it to run sometimes. On really bad nights he'd sleep in it."

"I heard he played football," she said, moving on to a happier subject.

"Quarterback." Larry smiled big, thinking back. "He got a couple of trophies. Even a scholarship to Georgia State."

Ella was surprised. "I didn't know he went to college."

Larry looked like he said something he shouldn't have. "Nah, he didn't go. He had an accident and wrecked his left arm. He was a left-handed quarterback," he explained. "he couldn't play football anymore."

She nodded her head. "I read about the Railroad Trestle accident, and how you were all almost killed by a freight train. That must have been terrifying."

Larry seemed surprised. "Not a lot of people know about it. Yeah, I have never been that scared before, or since. I have nightmares about it." He shook his head. "I don't even like to think about it."

"I'm sorry, Larry. Do you remember how my father reacted to it?" She was so close to knowing him, and understanding the decisions he made.

"Awful. It was horrible. Ray blamed himself for Skeeter's death, but it was an accident. Everybody said so. His arm was wrecked. His whole life, he carried the weight of Skeeter's death with him." Larry stopped and glanced at Ella. "He never got over it. Every time something good happened to him, he walked away. He thought he didn't deserve to be happy ever again."

She had to know. "Do you think that's why he left my mom and me? Because we were happy, and he didn't think he deserved a happy family?"

He nodded. "He told me so."

Tears welled up in her eyes, and ran down her cheeks. She tried to brush them away, she hated to cry. Especially with a black eye. It made her nose run, and it started to bleed again. "I'm a mess. Can you get me a tissue or something like that?"

Larry handed her a piece of a paper towel and she sopped everything up. "I'm so glad you told me. I was a little girl. I thought he left because I wasn't good enough."

He looked so sad. "Oh, no. I wish you could have met him and talked with him, like I did. You'd see that wasn't true."

She took a big sip of her tea, trying to wash her emotions away.

"Ray left Prosper, joined the army. He came back home about ten years later. Settled down. Worked as a football coach at the high school in Jessup for a while. Started woodworking after that." Larry looked at her. "We didn't spend much time together anymore, but he told me all about his daughter—you." She felt like a burden had been lifted, and smiled.

She drank the rest of her tea and moved on to the reason for her visit. "I came here to get some really important information from you, that I think only you know."

He looked worried. "I was afraid you were going to ask me about that."

"I interviewed Jake. I know you were at the bar with my father the night he was killed." Larry wouldn't look at her.

"He told me you were there, and he was pretty sure my father told you something, in confidence, about what he saw that afternoon. True?"

He nodded his head. "I wish he hadn't."

"I understand," she said. "It was something so bad that it got him killed later that night." She tried to get him to look her in the eye. "Is that why you left the bar?"

He shook his head, yes. "I wish he hadn't been there."

"Where was he?" Ella asked.

"Fishing down by the bridge," he said, quietly. He was looking out the window.

"Tell me. What did my father see?"

"A body being dumped in the river." It was an emotionless fact.

"Who did it?"

"It was Bud, I mean, Father Santos. And Bobby Dean, the cop."

Ella was silent. She guessed right on Father Santos, but Bobby Dean was a big surprise. "Are you sure?" She had to ask that.

"Yup. He saw them do it. Ray was sitting behind a tree so he thought he got away okay." He bit his lip. "He must've been wrong. They got to him pretty fast."

"You think one of them killed him?"

"Yes, ma'am." He stood up and took her empty glass into the kitchen. She rubbed the sides of her face, careful to avoid bruises and bumps. "Thank you for sharing this with me," she said, when he came back into the room.

He sat down and sighed. "If they find out I know about them, they'll kill me, too."

Ella was quiet. He was right. If they were arrested and it went to trial, Larry would have to testify. His life would be in danger.

He had a stubborn look on his face. "If you tell anybody what I told you just now, I'll flat out deny it. I don't know anything about it."

"Then you won't testify at a trial?"

"How could I?" he chuckled. "I don't know anything. Never saw anything."

While she understood his concern, and knew it was justified, she had hoped they could be arrested and tried for the crimes. Without Larry's testimony, it wouldn't happen. She sighed, and took a deep breath. Standing up, she extended her hand to him. "Thank you for your honesty. This conversation never happened."

He shook her hand. "Good luck. I have a feeling you're not going to stop here. Try not to get killed."

She smiled. "I've been lucky so far. If I can't arrest Father Santos, I can still have a talk with him, right?"

"Watch out," he warned. "I know Bud. He's not a nice guy. Don't let him fool you."

"They've killed two people so far. They are not nice guys." She was sure of that.

He pointed to her black eye and broken nose. "I'd like to see the other guy."

"You knew I must have been in a fight. You're right." She smiled. "The other guy will be easy to recognize," she said. "Four long, deep scratches on his cheek. And I'm going to find the son-of-a-bitch."

"I hope you do." He opened the screen door for her. She hugged him on her way out. "See you at Thanksgiving."

"Bring wine," he told her with a smile.

She started the long trek back to her car. It had been a very fruitful meeting and her mind was busy putting the pieces of the puzzle together. She didn't even feel the stinging nettle as she traipsed through the undergrowth. The mystery was almost complete.

Chapter 45
The Priest
Wednesday

The Catholic Church was on the way out of town, but still along the river. Ella parked her car with several others in the parking lot, hoping Father Santos would be inside.

She entered the vestibule cautiously, without her gun drawn, but easily accessible at her hip. In retrospect, it would have been a good idea to have Chief Jones come with her. *This is such a bad idea*, she thought. She tried to keep her hands from shaking by rubbing them together. She cautiously pushed open the doors to the nave, and looked around the large room. He was in the sanctuary arranging flowers in back of the altar and hadn't noticed her come in. She didn't see anyone else. She hoped Bobby Dean wasn't there.

She quietly walked halfway down the aisle then stopped by a pew on the right side. "Bud," she said, loudly. Then she repeated it.

He turned toward her, and smiled. "You must be the Chicago detective I've heard so much about. Welcome to our church." He lay the scissors down by the flowers and walked closer. "What on earth happened to your face?"

"Someone attacked me at my house yesterday. I think they're worried about what I might find out about the two murders in Prosper." She watched for his reaction.

He smiled. "That's just awful. It's a wonder you weren't killed."

"Yes, it's a wonder all right. My name is Ella Flynn. I've heard so much about you, Bud." He had an ominous, powerful presence.

"How did you know my name used to be Bud? I'm just curious."

She told him the truth. "I read an article about the Railroad Trestle train accident, and you were mentioned in it. I believe it said your name was Bud Santos before you became a priest. Is that right?"

"True, but not many people are aware of it. I'd prefer you call me Father Santos."

"Of course, Bud," she said. She watched him flinch. "I wanted to ask you a couple of questions, if you don't mind." She smiled.

He had walked to the edge of the platform. "That depends. About what?"

"I wanted to know if you knew a girl named Mary Ellen Bellacourt. She was recently found floating in the Altamaha River."

"Tragic," he said, without empathy. "We have a lot of activities for young people at the church. She could have participated in them. It doesn't have anything to do with me." He was staring at her.

"I have a picture if that would help." She took the picture out of her pocket and straightened it out. She walked to the platform and held it up so the Priest could see it.

"I might remember her," he said, shrugging his shoulders.

"Do you, or don't you?" she asked, without a smile.

"She looks familiar. I could have passed her in the hall a dozen times. I have no idea." He took a step down from the platform. It brought him even closer to Ella. He didn't take his eyes off her, and he didn't blink.

She backed up to the pew behind her, conscious of his strength and determination. She wasn't going to forget he was a murderer. "I think you knew her. I think you knew her well enough to kill her."

He was startled. "Are you insane? You think I killed her?" His benevolent demeanor suddenly changed to intimidation. His loud voice echoed in the church. "You can't be serious."

Ella was intensely aware she had unleashed a psychopath and he was coming her way. He was no longer rational. His anger was out of control as he screamed epithets at her. "How dare you say that," he screamed. Coming closer. "This is my church!"

Terrified, she grabbed her gun, held it up, and pointed it at the Priest. "Stop where you are," she shouted. "Don't come any closer or I'll shoot."

She took a quick step back, catching her foot on the carpet, twisting her ankle. She fell head first into the pew, fumbling for her gun, trying to stand back up. When she realized she wouldn't be able to get back up, she deftly tucked the gun into the waist of her jeans.

He had reached her and forced her face down on the wooden seat, his hand heavy on her back. "I'm going to make you sorry you said that, bitch." The words echoed around the room, bouncing off the walls and repeating themselves.

She was unable to move. She was trapped. She felt his knee on her back, his hands tightening around her throat. She couldn't fight back. This time there weren't any stars. Just blackness.

Chapter 46
In the River
Wednesday

When Ella regained consciousness, she panicked. She was in the car. In the river. *I'm drowning!* she screamed inside her head. She fought the urge to open her mouth and breathe in river water. *Air. I need air.* She was underwater. *I have to breathe! Drowning.* Cold, numbing water filled the car. Forcing the car farther down. Into the river. In the front seat of her car. Sinking into the river. Looking up at the ceiling. *Air pocket!* Pushing herself up to the car roof, sucking as much air as she could. Gasping. Her lungs burning. Trying not to cough. She needed control.

Sinking back into the water. Arms won't move. Zip ties on her wrists. The car groaning as it tips. *I've got to get out of here, now!* Nose down into the river. *The window!* Passenger side window. Partly open. Pushing up to the air pocket again. Taking in as much air as she could. Dropping back down in the water, grabbing the top of the window with her tied hands. Rocking the glass, back and forth, in and out. It was loose. Gathering her strength, bringing up her legs. *Kick it out!* Glass cracking, breaking away, giving way, a flood of cold river water. Gushing in. The car continuing to sink. The air pocket was gone.

Hands on the rearview mirror. Upside down. Feet first, out the open window. knocking out glass. Barely conscious, fighting for the light. Kicking off the car fender. Breaching the water. Sucking in fresh air. Violently coughing. Alive.

A tree limb from a fallen dead tree blocked her way into the current in the middle of the river. Stationary, immobile, she hung on to it, breathed and coughed until she was strong enough to fight for the shore. Using her hands together, she pulled herself, by gnarl and clumps of broken bark, until she reached the stump of the fallen tree. She stood up in the river mud sucking her shoes down into it. She pulled out one foot after the other until she reached dry land.

Bent over, retching, she watched her car in the river. The rear axle broke the water briefly, then continued its journey to the bottom of the river with a loud grinding noise. Several large bubbles came to the surface and popped noiselessly. Ella figured there must be thousands of cars at the bottom of the Altamaha River.

She walked a few more feet inland, took a deep breath, then like she had been taught, raised her zip-tied-wrists over her head as far as she could reach, and brought her arms down between her legs with as much strength as she could muster. The ties broke.

"Sonofabitch!" she screamed out loud. "Nobody told me it would hurt that much." She rubbed her raw wrists. She pulled her phone out of her pocket and tried to turn it on. Nothing. Nada. Zilch. She lobbed it into the middle of the river.

Solid land had never felt so good. She sat down in the grass and took her Converse hi-tops off to drain the water out and continued to complain loudly, all alone. "I got my ass kicked twice in two days. What the hell have I been doing for the past eight years? Have I learned nothing?"

She squeezed the water out of her socks and put them back on with her shoes. She was frustrated by her inability to fight back and angry with herself for not bringing Chief Jones. *I'm an idiot.* She had placed herself in a position of vulnerability. Her opponent was a psychopath, and she totally misjudged his level of insanity.

She would confront him again, alone, because she had no way to contact the Chief, no car, and she was way too angry to stop now. There was no evidence to arrest him, or Bobby Dean. Just one person's word against another's. It was up to her. They killed her father.

She found her gun still tucked into her waistband, and checked it out to make sure the ammo stayed dry. It did, but she'd have to be wary of a misfire. She put it back in its holster. Her khakis were made of a thin material, so they were already on their way to dryness, along with her big shirt.

The tape was not waterproof, so the nose splint was falling off. She ripped it completely off. "Ouch," she yelled. Her throat throbbed like it did the day before, even more bruised and swollen. Her hair was heavy with water. She squeezed it dry. Her nose had begun to bleed again, so she wiped the blood on her shirt.

Where is my Cubs hat? She located it wound around a section of her long hair behind her. She removed it carefully and put it back on, pulling her wet hair through the hole in the back.

She was alive, and that made her smile. She was also really pissed off. When she stood up, she was light-headed and dizzy and it took a few minutes for her to feel steady on her feet. There wasn't a spot on her body that didn't hurt. She stretched, up and around, until she felt more grounded. Ready to go.

Just out of sight of the highway, she walked parallel to the road, heading back toward the church. Ella didn't want to draw attention to herself, so she stayed behind the trees. Walking silently.

She could see the red roof edges of the church long before she reached it. When she finally got there, a gardener was on his knees weeding the garden that surrounded the sidewalk entry.

"How ya'll doing?" she asked, stopping to talk.

Surprised, he looked up at her. "Jesus, what happened to you?" He dropped his trowel in the dirt.

"I'm fine," she reassured him. "Do you know if Father Santos is in the church?"

"I believe he is, ma'am." The look on his face was painful. She thought it might be empathy.

"Do you have a phone on you?"

He felt his back pocket. "Yes, I do."

She wiped some blood off her nose with the back of her hand. "Do me a favor. In about ten minutes, call Chief Jones at the Prosper Police Department and tell him Ella said to get his ass over to the Catholic Church on 170. Stat."

"Yes ma'am. I'll do that."

"And one other thing."

"What's that?"

"Tell him to send an ambulance."

Chapter 47
Final Confrontation
Wednesday

For the second time that day, Ella entered the vestibule through the open doors to the nave. This time, though, the large room was empty, and this time, she had her Glock in her right hand, finger poised over the trigger. The church was quiet, except for the barest sound of activity beyond the sanctuary.

A hallway led to the back of the church. Soundlessly, with her back to the stained-glass windows, she moved steadily down the hallway, staying close to the wall. Gun drawn. Vigilant. She passed the Sacristy Room with vestments on a table, then noticed a door on the left slightly ajar. There was no one else in the vicinity. She quietly pushed the door open with her knee, holding her gun steady and pointed dead ahead.

Father Santos was writing in a ledger at a wood desk about ten feet from the door. He looked up at her, smiling a mirthless grin.

"Hi again," she said, pointing the gun at his head and walking into the room. "Surprised to see me?" Ella's heart was beating fast. She didn't feel nearly as confident as she sounded, she was trying hard to keep her hands from shaking.

"I wasn't expecting you." His voice was loud. "You have more lives than a cat," he said, returning to his ledger. "Put the gun away," he demanded, waving her away.

"No. I underestimated you once. I won't do it again." She stood her ground. "We weren't finished with our conversation, Bud."

"I was." His narrow eyes held a blank, unblinking stare. She felt him trying to bore into her soul.

"Tell me why you killed Mary Ellen," she said. "What did she ever do to you?"

He ignored the gun pointed at him. He seemed fearless. "Mary Ellen was a very stupid, stupid girl."

"What makes you say that?" Her arms were beginning to get heavy holding the gun.

He stopped looking at his ledger and sat back in his chair, staring at her. "She had the audacity to blame her pregnancy on me, a man of the cloth who stands head and shoulders above other men. A Priest. She was an irresponsible child."

Ella was stunned. Not an admission she anticipated. "Was it your child?"

"Young lady," he said to her, "this unborn child of hers could have had any number of fathers. She was a whore." He sneered when he said it. Like Mary Ellen had no value at all. Not to him.

She was surprised how easily he admitted he had sex with her. The Priest was a composite of all things Ella despised. Truly an evil person. "What did she want from you?" There had to be a quid pro quo.

"Why should I tell you?" He had a sinister smile.

She paused. "It would be my honor to shoot you, kill you right now. But I have a nagging curiosity about why you thought Mary Ellen had to be killed, her body dumped in the river." She wasn't kidding. She would do it.

"I'll tell you," he said, "but only because I can see Bobby Dean behind you, his gun aimed at your head. And his trigger finger much quicker than yours." He laughed out loud.

She glanced behind her and saw him.

"Now, put your gun down," the Priest demanded again. She hung her arms at her sides, numb, let her gun fall to the floor with a thud.

"Good girl," he smiled. "Why did I kill her? Because she was a stupid, stupid girl. She expected me to give her one-thousand dollars for her imaginary trip to New York, plus money for an abortion. She had previously tried to extort money from little Junior Wheeler and his daddy, the Mayor, and came up empty."

"You could have paid her off." Ella felt empty inside, the gun aimed at her, her life in the balance and no way out.

"Blackmail is never ending." His attention was waning, and he studied a picture on the wall. "She told me she would tell my congregation about my egregious acts if I didn't pay her off. I knew, even if I gave her the money, she would be back for more. It would be a never-ending cycle."

Ella didn't answer. Her knees were shaky and she felt sick. Bobby Dean was so close behind her, he wouldn't miss. She hoped it would be painless and quick.

"I shot her in the forehead. Didn't I, Bobby Dean?" She could see him nod his head out of the corner of her eye. "And we unceremoniously dumped her body in the river."

"My father saw you do that, didn't he?" She had to hear him say it.

"He did, indeed. Stupid, stupid man. Bobby Dean took care of that fly in the ointment." He motioned for Ella to come farther into the room so he could talk to Bobby Dean. He stood inside the doorway, his gun trained on her.

He began to mock the young man. "You're my little puppet, aren't you? The IQ of a potato. Tsk, tsk," he said. "I have never met anyone as stupid as Bobby Dean here. Incapable of making the most basic decisions. If it wasn't for me taking him in when he was a homeless child, he would have died. Nobody wanted him. Nobody." The Priest had become more animated as he chastised the man, he spoke faster and louder. Bobby Dean was stone-faced, but he would flinch with every insult.

"I told him to kill you, but he disobeyed me. You won't do that again, will you?" he said to Bobby Dean. It wasn't a question. It was a rebuke.

"He never thanked me," he said to them both. "That's why I took away his bird, twisted its neck, and left it in his bed."

Bobby Dean's eyes were large, angry, but he didn't say anything.

"I had to do it. How else would he learn?" He directed this question to Ella, seemingly waiting for her to agree with him.

The Priest was bored again. "Let's get this over with. We'll throw her body in the river with her car. She should have stayed there."

Ella looked at Bobby Dean, pleading with him. "Please don't do it. If you let me go, I won't tell anybody. I promise." Her voice had no inflection, she didn't have much hope.

"Bobby Dean, shoot her!" the Priest shouted. He smiled. "Do it!"

Bobby Dean didn't move.

Louder now, the Priest screamed at him. "How stupid are you? Obey me! Shoot her now!"

Bobby Dean glared at him, then changed the aim of his gun to the Priest's forehead. "No. You can't tell me what to do. Ever again."

There was a loud bang, and the Priest fell forward onto his desk, a pool of blood forming on the ledger. Bobby Dean dropped the gun, fell back into the hallway against the wall. His head in his hands.

Ella could hear the police siren outside drawing closer to the church. She picked up her gun and returned it to its holster, then sat in the closest chair. She was sure she could hear her heart beating in her ears. Breathing slowly, she bent over and quietly vomited on the floor.

Sounds of running in the hallway, then the Chief was in the

room with her. She could hardly hear him over the buzzing in her head. He knelt next to her chair, and put his arm around her. "Are you okay, Flynn?"

"Yes," she told him. "Bobby Dean shot the Priest." She pointed to the desk where he lay, face down on the ledger. "He told Bobby Dean to shoot me. He aimed a gun at my head. I thought I was going to die. But, he shot Father Santos instead." Ella was overwhelmed by what had happened, and how quickly it had ended. "I'm still alive," she said in disbelief.

"Yes, Flynn," the Chief said, patting her on the back. "You're still alive, thank God. I think you should get out of here, when you feel up to it, and go home. I'll come over later."

She remained in the chair. "Okay." She didn't make any attempt to move, she just breathed and stared ahead. More running footsteps in the hallway, and Jackson Lee was there.

He knelt beside her and checked her for injuries. He noticed the new bruising and redness on her neck. "Are you all right?"

She nodded her head. "I threw up on the floor."

"It doesn't matter," he said, glancing at the dead Priest. "As long as you're okay, nothing else matters." He helped her up. When she collapsed against him, he picked her up and carried her out to his car. He laid her down in the back seat and drove to the blue house.

Chapter 48
Bobby Dean's Confession
Wednesday Night

The church was a hive of activity. The police were all over the place, including paramedics attending the very dead priest with the Coroner hovering over them. The Crime Scene Investigation group was on the way.

Bobby Dean had been moved to another room, where he sat alone. Chief Jones stood at the door for a few minutes before walking in.

"Hey," he said, in a quiet voice.

The young man looked up, but didn't smile.

The Chief dragged a chair over to sit next to him. "When you told me you saw the burglar at Ray Flynn's house, that was a lie, wasn't it?"

He nodded. "Father Santos told me to say that. He wanted everybody to stop poking around in it."

"Why was that?"

He looked the Chief in the eye. "I did it. I killed him." The Chief noticed four long, deep scratches on his cheek.

"Yes, I thought so," he said. "You killed Ray. Was it the Priest's idea?"

"He told me I had to do it."

"Was it because Ray saw you and Father Santos put Mary Ellen's body in the river?"

"Yes, sir."

"Did you kill Mary Ellen, too?" He hated to ask this question.

"No, sir. He did it. He made me help."

"I understand," he said. "Thank you for telling me the truth, Bobby Dean. I'll leave you alone now." The Chief started to leave, then hesitated. "I'm glad you didn't shoot Detective Flynn. She's a really good person."

He didn't answer. Just stared into space.

Chapter 49
The Unraveling
Wednesday Night

The first thing Ella did was sleep. Then she took a long, hot bath. Her right eye was practically swollen shut and gravity had begun to pull her bruise down her cheek. Jackson Lee put another bandage and splint on her nose. The black-and-blue welts on her neck were new. Other than that, she thought she looked pretty good.

Walter greeted her with a loud series of howls. Where had she been? Why did she leave? What took so long? She patted him on the head. "Thanks, I love you, too."

The front room was full of people. Chief Jones, Connie, Mayor Big Dick, and Jim-Bob, the weekend cop. "Tomorrow I need you to come to the station to fill out a report," the Chief said. He pulled a chair in from the kitchen. Jackson Lee sat with his arm around Ella on the sofa. She patted an empty cushion, and Walter jumped up to join them.

"Just for my amusement," the Chief said, "tell me what happened today. Exactly."

Ella looked at Jackson Lee first, then the Chief. Her voice was raspy again. "Like I told you yesterday, I went to Larry's mom's house to find out how to locate him. Ida Pearl Taylor, a really lovely person."

"Focus," the Chief said.

She shook her head. "Sorry. She drew me a map, and even with the map, it was tough to find him. But I did." She smiled. She remembered how they talked about her father. She'd have to share it with Jackson Lee. "He told me that my father told him he was fishing down by the bridge, and saw two people dump a body in the river. He identified them as Father Santos, formerly Bud Santos, a childhood friend of my father's. And Bobby Dean. He was sure they murdered my father to keep him quiet."

The Chief glared at her. "You decided to confront men who had already killed two people, all by yourself. Do I have that part right?" He sounded angry.

"When you say it like that, it really sounds dumb."

He shook his head. "It was beyond dumb. It was ridiculous. Then what happened?"

"Larry told me he wouldn't testify at a trial because he thought they would kill him. His testimony would be hearsay, anyway. I couldn't arrest them because I'm not a cop anymore. They would be free to kill somebody else." She looked around the room at the people listening so raptly to her story. "I couldn't let that happen. They killed my father. They killed Mary Ellen. They had to be held accountable."

"You went into the church," the Chief said.

"I did. It went badly, that's all you need to know right now." *I'll tell Jackson Lee about it later.* "The next thing I knew, I woke up in my car, in the river, with my hands zip-tied in front of me." Connie gasped. Jackson Lee looked at her with wide eyes and disbelief.

Connie quickly distributed cans of beer, and tops were popped. Ella sat up and took a long drink. It was soothing on her throat. She tossed the can toward the garbage can. It went in. She high-fived Jackson Lee. She didn't burp, though, because she was a lady.

"Oh, my God," the Chief said. "I can't believe you're sitting in front of me right now. Were you trying to get killed?"

"No, I wasn't." She looked at Walter. He was tuned into her and seemed to know she was hurt. He licked her hand. "I was so angry. I wanted the Priest to tell me why he killed Mary Ellen, and why my father had to die. Obviously, I got out of the car in the river. I tried to dry out a little, but I still had my gun. I was so mad, I think I was numb to what might happen to me."

Everyone was quiet. "I went back into the church. I didn't see him, or anybody else, but I heard something down the hallway. With my gun drawn, I eased down the hallway and found Father Santos in his office. I pointed the gun at his head. He didn't seem to care at all. He was fearless." She was feeling very tired. "He told me he killed Mary Ellen because she tried to extort money from him, after she failed at getting money from Junior. Then, of course, they killed my father."

Mayor Big Dick Wheeler, who had been silent, chimed in. "Chief Jones told me you didn't think Junior was guilty, and to hold off on arresting him. I appreciate that, Flynn."

"I'm glad it worked out," she said.

"Also, I can tell you that your intruder was Bobby Dean. I saw the scratches on his face," the Chief said.

Ella wasn't surprised. "I figured that it was him."

"Are you finished for the night, Flynn?" the Chief asked, sarcastically. "Try to stay inside for now."

They got ready to leave, and Connie kissed her cheek. "I can't believe you were in the river."

"Me, either," she said, laughing. Then she remembered her car was still there. "I'm going to need a new car."

"Hold off on that," the Chief said with a smile. "I've got an opening in the police department I'd like to talk to you about."

"Really?" she said, smiling. "I think I'd like that."

"We'll talk about it later." He put his hat back on, and the group filed out the door.

Chapter 50
Wednesday night

"Has my father been cremated yet? Ella asked, timidly, when they were alone and sitting together on the sofa.

"Yes," Jackson Lee said. "I still have the ashes."

"I've changed my mind. I'd like to have his ashes with me."

Jackson Lee seemed surprised. "Yes, we can do that for you. What's changed?"

"Me," she said. "I'm not five anymore. He is my father, and always will be. I'm just sorry all those empty years got in the way. I would have loved to have gone fishing with him."

"Me, too," he said, smiling. "This is a good thing. A very good thing."

"Everything has changed, and yet I think I'm more me than I've ever been," Ella told him. "It's because of you. You are the funniest, kindest, finest man I've ever known." He had his arm around her shoulders. When he looked at her, she kissed him on the lips. He had to adjust his glasses. "When we first met, I didn't want to get involved with anyone. I didn't have the time or energy, and I didn't think I was ready for it. But you were so good to me, I got swept up and fell in love."

He smiled. "Stick with me. We're going to have a beautiful life."

Walter woke up and thumped his tail on the rug at their feet.

Jackson Lee's voice was hushed. "You are my home. I want to open up my life and bring you into it. Ella, I love you."

Then, for some perverse reason she couldn't understand, she started to cry. Her nose ran and it was painful. She sniffed, wiping her face off with the bottom of her shirt. Walter seemed concerned, and jumped on the sofa to stick his snout in her face. He began a low, droning whine.

Jackson Lee carefully removed the dog from her lap, and sat next to her. "I'm in it for the rest of my life," he told her. "I won't leave you." He kissed her like it was the first time all over again.

"I love you, too," she said. "You're all I need, and this is where I want to be."

ACKNOWLEDGMENTS

Detective Ella Flynn is a character created based on Chicago Police Officer Ella French, killed in the line of duty in 2021. She was a beautiful young woman with long dark hair, and she loved animals. *Don't call me Daughter* is my way of having her life continue. I know she would have enjoyed Walter and Jackson Lee Armstrong, and Prosper, Georgia.

ABOUT THE AUTHOR

Patricia Jean Childers

I live in a small town outside of Chicago with my husband, Chris, and dogs Roxy and Hunter. Hunter, a Bassett hound, is my muse and sits next to me in my recliner while I write. Roxy drips water, smells bad, and counter-surfs. Chris is a voracious reader and helped me with plotting and the storyline. If you don't like the book, it's his fault.

Made in the USA
Columbia, SC
20 September 2022

67215589R00126